Sin on a Broken Heart

SINS
BOOK TWO

RHIANNON FUTCH

Ebook ISBN: 978-1-955749-01-5

Print ISBN: 978-1-955749-27-5

Cover by sunsetrosebooks.com

Editing by V. Editing Services

Contents

One

Jasmine

Chloe puts the car in park, we get out to take a good look at the house the three of us now own. It is a two story colonial style, but with more space. Rather plain on the outside but we don't mind. It is better for us if we live in a place that doesn't draw attention. After all, three vampire women are bound to draw attention, better if it doesn't start early with the house.

Scarlett pulls into the drive while we are standing there staring. She pops up out of her car and says, "What are you waiting for? Let's go inside! It should be furnished, so we just need to bring in our things. I want to walk through first though."

Chloe shrugs, "Let's do it. I'm starved. I think after we tour the place I am throwing my stuff in my bedroom and heading for Club Five."

Club Five is Chloe's favorite hunting ground. She get a thrill out of seeing the guys faces when the hunter becomes prey. She tells me it is like an adrenalin rush for her. I can definitely see the draw. The few times I have gone with her were fun. She has a knack for choosing the guys that are predatory, the ones looking for a woman to abuse. Those are her favorites, the worse they are the more she wants to drain them dry. I have taken to keeping a spell on the dumpsters there, to keep people from finding the bodies while they are near her hunting ground. Just a little something to keep them unseen until they are long gone from the area.

Scarlett unlocks the front door and we walk in to a very suburban house. The furniture is all quite floral as are the curtains. There are live, laugh, love stickers on the wall in the kitchen. I raise my brows at Scarlett as she and I watch Chloe snatch the stickers off the wall. She balls them up and tosses them into the trash bin. She looks up to find us watching, "What? I hate those stickers. The flowers are going to have to go to, but I think I can hold off on violence to the drapery until we get some new ones."

We grin at her as she pushes through us and heads for the stairs. The staircase is pretty grand, dark wood with a green runner. The second floor branches to the left and right. We go to the left opening doors and peeking in each. The first is an office, the next two are bedrooms. One on each side of the hall. I decide I want the one on the back corner, it has a bathroom and I like the view, I'll be able to see the moon rise most nights. The room across from mine is roughly the same but a different view. We head for the far side of the hall to find two more offices and two more bedrooms. Chloe and Scarlett claim those, as they are both larger bedrooms, each with their own ensuite. I hear someone knocking and head downstairs, telling Scarlett and Chloe it is probably Leonidas's wolves with my stuff.

Downstairs I open the door to find the same wolf that told me I smelled good. I snap my teeth at him and he grins,

"Watch it ma'am, I bite back. Where do you want your things?"

I laugh, "Oh no, I just hate being bitten... Upstairs to the left, last room on the right."

He is still chuckling and shaking his head at me as he walks back to the truck parked in front of our house. I walk back upstairs to find Chloe and Scarlett, they are just coming out of Chloe's room, Scarlett looks over at me and says, "Chloe got the short stick on a closet. We were talking about opening the office next to to it and turn that into a closet. We could actually do that for all the bedrooms. What do you think?"

"I like it. It would give us each more of our own private space. It was the wolves at the door, they are bringing my bed up now."

The guy I snapped at yells up, "If we were wolves at your door it would really give the neighbors watching the wrong impression. Karen is standing on the sidewalk, she looks like she wants to call the HOA manager."

"Good thing we don't have an HOA. Karen can eat a dick." I look at Scarlett and Chloe, "Do you all want to take care of her?"

Chloe shakes her head no as she rubs her stomach, "Probably won't make us popular with the neighbors if I eat her."

Scarlett laughs, "Depends on whether or not she has been pissing off the entire neighborhood, they might throw you a party."

I shrug, "Ok, I'll go talk to her. I don't know if that is going to make things better though."

I head down the stairs and out the front door to find Karen trying to question the guys as they carry in a lot more things than I should have. Leonidas and I are going to have to have a talk about this. I walk up and step between her and the wolf, forcing her to step back as I put on my cheery customer service persona, "Hi there, neighbor! So nice to meet you! My name is Jasmine, what's yours?"

I thrust my hand out at her and watch as her eyes travel down my body, her lip curling in disgust. I look down and remember I am wearing cutoff shorts with fishnet stockings, boots, and a Slipknot crop top. Oh well, better Karen understands from the start. She takes my hand with her fingers and I push in for a full hand shake as she says, "My name is Karen. I am the unofficial neighborhood organizer," she took her hand from mine to make little air quotes around the word unofficial. I watch as she wipes her hand on her slacks, "I try to get to know everyone that lives on this street, so we can all work together to maintain our property values."

I chuckle and put my hands in my back pockets, thrusting my chest out. I hear one of the wolves say, "Fucking hell!" under his breath and I try not to laugh. "Well, Karen, huh, that's really your name? Wow. Okay, well. Going to guess you don't like large pink flamingos or year round Halloween decorations or gargoyles. Which is really unfortunate, as I just adore all those things and so do my girl friends."

She gasps, "Girlfriends? What?" She glances at the house and back to me, "Are you saying you're all..." She swallows and then whispers, "lesbians?"

I laugh, "Oh honey, it won't make it less likely if you whisper it. And though it isn't any of your business, no. We aren't lesbians. We are all bisexual though. Are you feeling a little frustrated? Is your husband not quite getting you there? I could introduce you to some competent professionals, but we don't do that."

Karen has started to back away from me, her mouth hanging open and her hand clutching for pearls she isn't wearing right now, "You godless women stay away from me! You devil women are ringing Satan's doorbell and he is going to answer! You get out of this neighborhood! This is a good, god-fearing place and we don't need your kind inviting evil!" She turns and runs home, her little ballet flats tapping across the street and down two houses before she gets to her house and rushes in, slamming the door behind her like I was chasing her.

I hear the wolves behind me laughing and I turn, "Say, what are your names? And, what is all this extra stuff?"

The one I have been talking to walks over to sit on the edge of the truck, "I am Banner," he jerks a thumb towards the others, "these are Dario, Mario, and Elliot. As for the stuff, well, boss said to tell you that you should have things so he went shopping for you and it is all gifts. No returns."

I am stunned. He bought me things just because he thinks I should have stuff? What's the catch? "What? Why did he buy me things? What did he buy me? Why didn't he tell me?"

Banner ticks off reasons on one hand as he lists them, "He bought you things because you deserve better than you think you do. He bought a variety of things with an emphasis on books. He didn't tell you so you couldn't veto the idea and because he is counting on you not wanting to be mean to us as a way to keep you from giving it back."

"How would I be mean to you if I gave it back?"

"If you want it to go back to him then we have to carry it."

"Why?" I ask as I cross my arms under my breasts and narrow my eyes.

He looks concerned for his health as he says, "Because that's what our boss said. He said if you don't want it we have to carry it all back out. And I have to tell you Jasmine, it is hot as hell out here. Wolves run hotter anyway, so this heat is brutal. We would really like to not carry it all back out."

"Oh hell, I didn't know that! You all keep a higher body temperature? All right, the stuff can stay. You lot, go get some air conditioning. Thank you for moving all the things, come give me a hug."

Banner hops down to get his hug first, it starts with a normal hug until he realizes that vampire skin is always cold and he straightens, holding me tightly to him as he lifts me off the ground. "Holy shit guys, she is cold! I didn't know vampires were cold, damn shame you are seeing the boss, I think I could get down with a vampire." He presses his face into the side of my neck and my legs wrap around his waist of their own volition. He seems to come to and pulls his head back, "I should put you down, Karen is probably calling the police right now about the lewd display." I laugh as I drop my legs from around his waist. He sets me down and then stands behind me as the other three hop out of the truck and collect their hugs. Each one presses close upon finding me still blessedly cool to the touch as Dario put it.

Banner collects one more quick hug, saying the other one wore off, before he hops in the truck and they leave. I walk back in the house with an extra sway to my hips just for Karen because I can feel her beady eyes on me.

Closing the door behind me I see Chloe and Scarlett over at the window, still looking out. They motion for me to come look and they point toward Karen's house. It would appear that Karen was prepared for scary, godless women. As she now has her husband putting up yard signs... Super. Well, I guess the neighborhood will be leaving us off the potluck list. Probably better that way.

* * *

Leonidas

. . .

I watch as everyone gets themselves sorted. The small warehouse we use for a clubhouse of sorts has seen better days. I am disgusted by the way it looks. I didn't care about anything for so long and then Jasmine. That night I took everyone out for a feeding party, it must have been fate. I didn't even feed that night. When I saw her driving up in that clunker I thought she must be insane. When she told me to fuck off right before she ducked under the trailer to run, I was hooked. I could see in her eyes that she knew she was done for but she wasn't willing to give up. If Mikael hadn't taken her with him that night, I would have turned her myself. I look around the room, they are as settled in as they are going to get. I know they won't all like the changes I have planned but as I look out over my little gang I know there are none that could beat me.

"All right, shut up so I can speak. It's time for some changes here. A restructuring. The gang life isn't for me anymore," most of them start shouting what about them and how are they going to get by without their family. And that is exactly where I want them going with this. "Quiet!" I wait until every sound in the building has stopped before I continue, "We are going to move out of being a gang and into being a family, a clan if you will. Acting like a gang and being vampire is only going to get us discovered and either killed or turned into science projects. I am still head of the family and you will do as I say or get out.

Speaking of getting out, if you don't want to be part of the clan you can leave, with no ill will and with some money to start over wherever you decide to stay." A low hum of conversation begins and I wait it out. As they go silent again I tell them, "Those of you that stick around, I have big, legal things planned and we will all profit from it with a lot less work and better hours. We are phasing out the drugs and starting a construction firm. I already have a successful one that has, until now, only worked during the day. However, with a lot of vampires on the crew and working at night, we can build much faster. Now, are you with me or are you out?"

The room explodes into shouts and cries, fuck, this lot can be so dramatic sometimes.

Mikael

That fucking bitch. Leaving me here to rot when she could have done the decent thing and died like a good woman would have. No, she fought and managed to catch me off guard. Now I am left here to heal while she is out there getting into who knows what.

Picking up the damn bell and giving it a shake, I hear Vigo running this way. He has been so much better an assistant than any I have had previously. He appears in the doorway and steps into the room, head bowed, "How can I serve you sir?"

"I need blood again. I have to feed more than usual if I am to get the use of my legs back again. Bring me two bags this time. I can move my big toe after the last two. I also need my laptop from downstairs, I need to go over some information in it before I make my next move."

"Move, sir?"

"Yes Vigo, my next move. Even stuck here to heal I am

working to exact my revenge on the bitch that did this to me. Go get what I need and stop your time wasting!"

Vigo takes off at a run and I yell, "Don't break the laptop!"

Long minutes later he returns with bags of blood and my laptop. He sets the laptop on the nightstand and hands me a bag of blood with a napkin. I bite into the bag and begin to drink, my thirst is like one trapped in the desert with no oasis in sight ever since she drained me nearly to death while I was so injured. How did she manage to throw me like that? I am certain she doesn't have that kind of strength in her. Maybe I was just off my game because it hurt so much to be forced to kill her like that?

Vigo bustles back over as I finish the first bag and sets a small tray over my useless legs before taking the empty bag from me and replacing it with the fresh. He places the laptop on the tray and asks, "Is there anything else you require sir?"

"No, this is fine for now. I will ring when I need more."

He backs out of the room and I am reminded of the old days when servants and women both acted better. Women died when they were killed and servants were a dime a dozen. Happy to have the smallest of what they considered luxuries. I think Vigo could be that kind of servant given the proper training. Continuing to drink from the bag I open the laptop and type in my password.

I had an investigator find out everything possible about each of Leonidas's gang members a few years back and knowing who each one is has made it too easy to continue to track them. Scrolling slowly through the information within I make notes on some likely contacts. I need someone in Leonidas's circle so I can destroy his relationship with her. But first, I need to find out where she is hiding. Pulling up the contacts on my phone I find my current favorite investigator and tap the screen to call him.

Three

Jasmine

The sun has no effect on me but I still wake as it goes down, the vampire in me knows the rising and setting of the sun and I feel it whether I need to or not. Stretching I feel something tickling me all over and I throw myself out of the bed to land in a heap on the floor. What fucking bugs crawled into my bed while I was sleeping? The floor feels weird too, I am about to have a full on panic attack over this shit, I am trying to keep breathing as I make my way to the light switch. I can see what looks like roots all over my floor. Flipping the light switch I see that my room is filled with ivy! How? What would... Oh no. Oh no. I did this. My magic is running amok again. How do I stop this? Oh no, they are still growing. I dash over to my nearly covered nightstand to grab my phone and get out of the room. I shut the door behind me, hoping the ivy will stay in there? Maybe? I need to call Helen. Stumbling my way downstairs as I pull up her name in my phone. Hitting the call button I pace the entry while it rings. Helen finally answers, "Hi Jasmine! How are you?"

"Not good, not good. I seem to have called some vines into my room while I was sleeping? Oh man," I see the vines moving slowly down the stairs, "they are still coming. Can you come over and help me stop this?"

"Wait, they are moving as you watch? This isn't a vampire eye sight thing? I will be able to see them?"

"You will be able to see them move. So will you come?"

"Yes. I think I need to see this."

* * *

I pace the entry area as I wait. The vines are growing steadily, they have made it down five steps already. I hear Chloe and Scarlett emerge from their bedrooms. Shit. I am going to have to tell them. I hope they don't decide I need to move out over this. What if they don't want anything to do with a vampire that has uncontrolled magic? Or worse, what if they think I am an abomination? They might decide I need to die.

I stop pacing as they step over vines on their way down the stairs. Scarlett says, "Care to explain why we have vines growing in the house and down the stairs? Since they do appear to come from your bedroom."

I run a hand across the back of my neck, "Well. I have been keeping a couple secrets from everyone. The one that is real important right now is that I have magic. It came from Mikael, he had it all this time but it is different with me. If seers are to be believed, they were meant for me the whole time anyway."

Chloe and Scarlett cross their arms in front of themselves. Chloe asks, "Why haven't you told us this before now? Why did we have to find out because vines were creeping down the hall?"

"I know, I know. I'm sorry. When I was first turned Mikael told me he would kill me if I told anyone else about the magic or the other thing. His warning kind of stuck and I still find myself reluctant to tell anyone. And if I am really honest, I didn't know if you would still want me around if you knew. Or if you would think I was an abomination that needed to be killed."

Scarlett and Chloe look at each other, their brows scrunched down and frowns on their lips. Scarlett takes the lead saying, "Honey, we would never—"

"Wait," I hold up my hand palm out, "before you say anything else, there is more. Another thing that I don't know for sure will be tolerated by any vampire. This one, this one is probably dangerous just to know. So, before I tell you, do you want to take that risk?"

Chloe bites her lip, "Do you have anything else that you haven't told us?"

"Just assorted shady things from my past. But nothing like these."

They share a look and then look to me, nodding yes. I take a deep breath, "The sun has no effect on me."

Scarlett's brows raise, "Girl, that isn't possible. What is the real secret?"

"I swear to you, it's true. And what's worse is that I accidentally passed it on to Leonidas. I got it from Mikael, same as the magic. He can walk in the sun too. Remember when he brought me home? We drove to his house in the sunlight. Didn't you wonder how I got there and had gotten some sleep already when you woke up that night?"

I watch as their eyes widen, Scarlett asks, "Has Leonidas passed it on to anyone?"

"Not that I know of. It only seems to pass through blood. I don't know how far it can be passed. I don't know much of anything about it except that I can walk in the sun. I generally don't because I worry about the wrong people figuring it out."

Chloe nods, "So you got magic and immunity to the sun from Mikael, did you pass both on to Leonidas?"

"No. My teacher taught me to sense magic in others, he doesn't have any."

"He got the immunity to the sunlight and nothing else," Chloe paces a bit, "I am guessing it happened during sex, since you said passing it to him was accidental. Which means it takes very little of your blood to effect that change. And he hasn't been bit by anyone other than you since then. Is that because he didn't want to pass it on or because he hasn't wanted to have sex with anyone else?"

I hear Helen's car door slam as do my friends, "That will be Helen, she is the one teaching me to control my magic. Don't blame her that I am a bad student. She tries. I think more the first one, he doesn't want to pass it on."

I open the front door before Helen can knock and pull her inside before Karen down the street can get a good look at her. She is flustered as I close the door behind her, "Young lady! You absolutely do not manhandle your teacher! I am old and human! We break."

"I'm sorry, Karen down the street is watching and I didn't want her to get a good look at you. She is too nosy and rude for her own good."

Helen rubs her temples, "Wonderful. And who are these lovely ladies?"

I wave a hand in Scarlett's direction, "The one with the dark hair and darker eyes is Scarlett and the one with the neon hair," I say as I gesture toward her, "is Chloe. They are vampires as well as my room mates and dear friends who now know all my big secrets."

Helen raises her brows, "Oh my." Her eyes flick to the

staircase and stay. Her hand slowly moves to cover her mouth which is now hanging open. "I can see them growning. They are moving right now." She turns to me, "Why haven't you shielded to get your magic contained?"

"You didn't tell me I should! Is that all I need to do?"

"Sort of. It is the place to start. No go on, do it."

I focus on shielding myself, on creating a sort of energy egg around myself to keep my magic from spilling out and wreaking havoc like this. Helen watches the vines as I work, clapping her hands together when they stop growing.

Four

Jasmine

"Excellent! You did great in stopping it, I dare say you could have done so before I arrived though I am glad to have gotten to see it. I would not have believed they could be made to grow so quickly, especially by someone with so little training..." Helen drifts off into silence as she stares at the vines.

We all wait for her to start speaking again but she just stares at those vines, a frown spreading across her face. "Um, how do I get rid of them?"

My question startles Helen and she jumps, her hand going to her heart, "Oh! Well, there are spells but they are too advanced for you. You have to be able to continually maintain control of your power before I can teach you that. And, as your teacher in the craft, I feel like hauling out the mess you created will be a great way to keep you mindful of your power." She walks across the room and takes my hands in hers, "I need you to understand that this could have been so much worse. You are," she glances at the vines, "or least were, so much stronger in fire. What if your power had set the place on fire? You and your friends could have died."

I am horrified, "It never occurred to me that I could accidentally hurt anyone. Oh god, oh, I'm not safe to be around."

Helen snatches my hands, bringing my attention squarely back to her, "You listen to me! Yes, this absolutely could have been bad. I very much want you to remember that. But I also want you to keep in mind that this is something you were made to be. You were always meant to have this power. Magic doesn't seek out random people. Not ever. It goes where a home for it was always intended to be. You can control your magic, you just need practice. I am going to give you some exercises to practice, things that will help you to have your magic under control always. You take this as your warning. That's all. Your magic is trying to help you. Help you to remember the responsibility that comes with having magic. You are not the first little witch to have an accident, nor will you be the last. Understand?"

I draw a shaky breath as she finishes, "You promise? What if this is bigger than me? Maybe it wasn't meant for me and it is all a big mistake."

Helen releases my hands and wraps her arms around me, hugging me tight as she tells me, "Little one, nothing about you is a mistake. You are made for this. Trust in yourself and do the work. It will all work out." She releases me and peers into my eyes, I don't know what she sees in there but she nods. "Well, now that there is manual labor to be done I have pressing business to attend to right now. I will have a new test for you on Wednesday." She rubs her belly, "And I see tacos in my very near future. Wonderful to meet you all, do stop by the book store, we are open 24 hours a day and accept all who will behave. Bye!"

She has the door open and closed behind her before I can

even say good-bye. I think she really wanted nothing to do with helping take care of these vines. I look to Chloe and Scarlett, they look a little shell shocked. I ask them, "Are you okay? Do you need me to leave the house for a little while?"

My question snaps them back and they glare at me. Chloe snarls, "No we don't need you to leave the house! Ugh! You are our friend, we aren't getting rid of you for being different or more. Fool. It is just a lot to take in. When your teacher arrived and gave you instructions while watching the vines, it just made it a little more real is all. I don't know about Scarlett but I was willing to think that you were mistaken and it would be explained some other way later when new evidence came to light."

Scarlett nods, "Exactly. And now, now it kind of has me thinking about the sun..."

Chloe's eyes go big and round, "The sun. If she— We could— Holy shit." She slumps down to the floor, her hands over her mouth.

Scarlett looks up from Chloe, "It's true, what you said, isn't it? You can go out in the sun, can't you?"

I wrap my arms around myself, "I can."

Scarlett nods and Chloe says, "I need to see it. And then, would you maybe? I shouldn't ask. You're right, if this gets out, other vampires will want you dead. If you gave it, it would put a target on our backs if it gets out." She shrugs, "Who am I kidding? If it gets out that you can be out in the sun, all our lives will be forfeit anyway, simply for the suspicion that you might have shared it with us."

I nod, "I can go. I have money, I can find another place so you will be safe. I don't want— I never wanted to put you in danger. I didn't think this through either. I'll get the vines and I'll find another place. I can't stay here and endanger you with my reckless behavior."

I start for the stairs but Scarlett and Chloe stop me, by appearing directly in front of me. Scarlett says, "What the hell is wrong with you? You are our friend. Being in danger is part of the vampire package. Other vampires frequently try to kill each other. Hell, there are three or four lurking about that I still owe damage to, but haven't seen around. You being able to walk in the sun is dangerous, but also wondrous. I would give a lot to be able to feel the sun on my skin again without catching fire. I have been vampire for nearly five thousand years. Where I lived, the sun was so bright it could blind you. We worshipped it as the symbol of one of our gods. I don't care about the danger it puts me in nearly as much as I care about sitting in the sun again."

Chloe slips an arm around Scarlett and gives her a squeeze, "Scarlett is right, on both counts. I have been vampire for even longer, though where I was we women were kept away from the sun. Not that it did any good to have us so sheltered when the head of our family invited the vampire to dinner. I too would do terrible things just to feel the warmth of the sun on my body again. Do not fear putting us in danger for such a wondrous gift as you have. I want to see it. I want to see you in the sun. And then, then I will beg for the gift you have been given, danger be damned."

I had never heard Chloe speak so formally or with the slight accent, an accent that spoke not of any one language so much as it spoke of the memory of many. My heart is full to overflowing with the idea that they would want me to stay even with the added danger I present. I know that the possibility of being able to be in the sun is a part of it, but they could seek that from me without keeping me around. "I, I don't know what to say. I will definitely give you a demonstration as soon as possible. But," I wrap my arms around myself, "are you sure you want me to continue to stay here? I could still give you the ability and no one would be the wiser without you around me unless you slip up."

They say in unison, "We are sure."

Scarlett chuckles, "With or without the ability to be in the sun, you are important to us. You are part of our vampire clan. Besides, how are we going to continue to tweak Mikael's nose if you leave?"

I laugh, "I guess there is that. Okay. I mean, if you are sure..." They both glare at me, "I won't bring it up again. You are very much stuck with me now," I tell them as I throw my arms around the two of them and pull them in for a hug.

Five

Leonidas

I watch for long minutes as they argue among themselves. What was I thinking, letting them go like this? They have no discipline and very little sense right now. Just a lot of amped up egos and with an even larger sense of entitlement. I grow tired of the noise and I loudly project my voice so it will carry throughout the warehouse over all other noise, "QUIET!"

Silence falls so quickly we are left with echoes of my voice. I let them soak in the power of my voice for a beat. "Now that you all can hear the rest of what I came here to tell you, I will continue. As I am changing things drastically, I will let those who do not wish to stay leave. No consequences. Any that leave will receive a lump sum as a severance package of sorts."

One voice rises from the back of the room, "What if we don't want to leave? What if we like things just how they are? Maybe you should leave."

I hear the edge to Craigo's voice, I know he is going to

challenge me. "Craigo, You don't want to do this. If you challenge me you forfeit any possible severance and your life. Take the money and walk away."

"Fuck you Leo!" Falon shouts, "I challenge you. The three of us challenge you. You lead like shit, always holding us back when we were obviously meant to rule this world. Humans are nothing more than fodder! Your insistence on not slaughtering them as we please is over, when we run the gang their will be no severance because no one is leaving."

Bobby steps forward, "But we can be magnanimous. If you would like to step down as leader, we'll probably let you leave with your life." His grin is cocky as he elbows Craigo and they laugh.

I shake my head. Idiots. They have barely ten years as vampires between them. The only ones they are stronger than are humans and newer vampires. Shrugging out of my jacket I ask, "Are there any others that feel this way?" Looking around I see vampires backing away, shaking their heads no. Ben and Haw have stayed next to me the entire time, turning to stand beside me in a show of solidarity as soon as they knew what I was up to. "I will fight you each, one after the other. Ben, Haw, I ask that you ensure it remain one on one. Nothing more. Are we clear?"

The three of them saunter up, I watch as they decide which of them will face me first. Ben and Haw step forward and turn to face me, keeping the three idiots in their peripheral vision, Ben tells me, "We are with you. Wherever you lead we are with you. We will keep this one on one, the only thing we ask is to be your second in command."

The two of them are the most honorable members of my gang, each is much older than I am but neither one has any desire to lead. I couldn't do any better for second in command if I tried, "Done. You are both my seconds in command, your job to keep the clan together and safe above everything else. Now, I have heads to detach. We'll continue this conversation after I finish this." Tossing my jacket at a chair behind me I walk forward into the open space created when everyone backed away.

Craigo is the first to enter the space with me. His arrogance is due mostly to his size, he is a big bastard. But he is also slow and his skills at fighting are poor. He is used to bullying people into doing his bidding. He struts over to stand before me, "Ready to concede yet, Leo?"

"Not a chance. Shoot your shot Craigo." He swings on me, his meaty fist missing me by a mile as I slide to the left and hammer his ribs with a flurry of rib breaking hits. The sound of bones grinding fills the space between us as he pulls back, trying to regain his balance. I keep moving, circling him and leaning back out of reach as he swings his arm back blindly. He turns with the momentum of his swing, his other hand telegraphing his plans. As he leans into the swing I kick his knee, turning it in a way knees were never meant to turn. He crashes to the ground and I stomp on his chest caving it in, dancing back out of reach before he can grab me. As he struggles to roll over I ask him, "Will you concede?"

He pauses in his struggle to flip me off, not being able to speak with his airways cut off. I shrug, "So be it then." I walk over to stand just above his head, his eyes widen and fear creeps in as I lean down he starts to bring his arms up to defend himself but I am faster and I grasp his head, twisting and snatching it from his body in a spray of blood. I toss the head off to the side as I straighten. Wiping away the blood on my face I say, "Who's next?"

Falon laughs, "That would be me." His steps are like a

dancer, each one placed very deliberately though all his focus seems to be on me.

We circle each other, as my back faces Bobby, Haw rushes forward and I duck in time to avoid the slash of Bobby's knife. Falon kicks out at me and I grab his foot, using his own momentum to throw him back as I stand. He hits the ground a few feet away and a spray of blood hits my back. I step to the side to see what is happening behind me while keeping an eye on Falon. Haw tosses Bobby's hand, still gripping the knife to the ground. Bobby shouts, "What the fuck are you doing Haw? I nearly had him! The gang would be free to be the kings we are without him."

Haw shakes his head, "No stupid. We would be free to expose the vampire community and become dust like your friend over there. What do you think the council will do when you start running amok calling yourselves kings and killing as you please? They send the exterminators to kill the roaches, that's what. Then your little white ass will be nothing more than so much dust in the breeze."

Bobby's eyes grow round, "There is no such thing as the council! That's just a fairytale told to keep us in line."

Haw chuckles, "You tell yourself what you need to dumb-ass. But you are going to wait your turn to fight him. Maybe your hand will be partially grown back by the time he gets done with Falon."

Falon chooses that moment to throw a chair at me, I snatch it out of the air as he charges and swing it round to bring it crashing down on his spine, snapping it as parts of the metal chair are embedded in his spine. He falls to the ground at my feet, face down as I reach down and twist-snatch his head from his shoulders. Another spray of blood hits me. I straighten and toss the head off to the side. Grinning at Bobby

I wipe some of the blood from my eyes, "Ready when you are."

Haw chuckles as he walks away from the fight. Bobby's eyes dart around, looking for help in the crowd. Ben and Haw are watching the crowd as well, eyes narrowed and stances ready to leap at anyone moving to help Bobby. No one moves and the ones I can see turn their eyes away as Bobby looks for help. Holding his dripping arm stump to his body he says, "It won't be a fair fight anymore," his mouth twists with a sly smile, "your henchman took my hand. We'll have to reschedule."

I smile at him as I lick some of Falon's blood from my lips, "You lost your hand trying to ambush me. You don't get to reschedule. Your life is forfeit unless you can beat me."

He flings blood at me, gesturing with his stump to hide the other arm reaching back for a weapon hidden on him, "This is why you shouldn't lead! You're unfit! A vicious killer interested only in hoarding power for yourself!"

He pulls a gun from behind him and levels it at me, emptying the clip into my chest. I laugh as he shoots. He tries to hit my head with the gun as I tackle him to the ground, but he misses, hitting my shoulder. We land, sliding a few feet with the momentum of my leap, and I scramble to sit on his chest, pinning his arms with my legs. One more twist and snatch, blood sprays the vampires standing in front of us.

I toss his head off to the side as I stand. "Any-fucking-body else want to throw a challenge?" I look around and see lots of head shaking and backing away. "Good. Figure out what you want to do. Stay or go, let Haw and Ben know your choice and don't make me rip any more fucking heads off tonight."

* * *

"How many?" I wait while they count the totals on the sheets they had them sign. One for stay and one for go. Simple and to the point. The sheet for stay looks from here like it has more signatures. Surprising really, as I would have sworn that at least half of them were going to leave before the fights.

I need to feed soon. The taste of their blood has me hungry for more and a bag isn't going to do it tonight. Tonight, I hunt.

Ben looks up from the paper in his hands, "Ten staying, counting Haw and myself."

Haw says, "Five gone, eight if you count Craigo, Falon, and Bobby. Daphne left and I have never been so glad to see a woman leave."

Haw has an easy time with women, always keeping their expectations low and never staying with any one so to hear him say that about one is odd. "Why? You usually like women to wander in and out of your space."

"Never her. She just gives me a feeling like I would be taking a snake to bed. It might be fun for a minute but you are definitely going to get bitten by that snake." Haw shudders, "She always looks like she is calculating what she can get from everyone and how she can burn them. I don't feel comfortable around her."

Nodding I turn to face them, "I am going out to hunt. All the blood earlier has left me hungry for fresh. Here are keys to the new place. I'll text you the address. Go, pick your rooms. My stuff is in the upstairs master. You being my seconds, you get first pick of any other rooms. We will be adding on, but some will need to share at first. You two do not have to share unless you choose to do so." Handing over the keys I walk out of the warehouse and toward my truck only to find some asshole flattened my tires.

Ben and Haw walk up behind me, "Need a ride?"

"Looks like. I'll send a truck to get this tomorrow. Drop me off in the downtown area."

* * *

Leonidas

Ben dropped me off at the edge fo the downtown area. I walk the streets slowly, looking for my mark. I see some women walking home from work, others in drunken groups wandering to the next bar. I am not interested in any of them. Then I see the one. He is following a pair of women. They look and smell nervous, their pace quickening as he draws closer to them. I nod to them as they pass, then walk casually across the street to intercept him.

"Hello friend," I greet him as I step into his path. He was so focused on the women that he never saw me coming. He grunts at me and tries to step around. I grab his arm and hold him in place.

He focuses on me, "They're getting away! Dammit! What the hell do you want?"

I let a smile spread slow across my lips, "I want to talk to you about a better hunting opportunity. You look like a hunting man, tracking your prey like you were. I know where to find a..." I inhale, smelling his excitement at the prospect. Oh, I picked the right one, "a better mark."

He is nearly drooling at the prospect, "I'm in! Where?"

I slip an arm around his shoulders and lead him toward the park, "This way friend, we keep these games to the shadows. Less likely to get caught, you understand, don't you?"

He begins to babble on about how hard it is to hunt a woman properly these days. He isn't the least bit concerned as

I take him into the darker parts of the park. We get to a nice secluded area and I release him to scent the air, making sure there are no others around that might spoil my fun. He begins to get nervous now, I can smell the fear growing in him as he asks, "Where is she?"

I turn toward him, my fangs lengthening as I smile, "Oh friend, you understand I'm sure."

He screams and turns to run but I am on him before he can take a step. He trembles in my grip as I dine on his fear, inhaling deeply. "Wha- what are you going to do to me?"

I laugh, "I'm just going to have a bite. Don't worry, you'll like it." I force his head to the side and lean in to his neck, the pulse in there is frantic. Sinking my teeth into his flesh I drink deeply, his hot blood courses through me, sating the hunger caused by the fights. He is moaning now and his pelvis is thrusting weakly at me. I drain him dry and lick the wounds to seal them. I let his now limp body fall to the ground. Looking around I realize I did not think this through. Hunger had me searching for a convenient spot to feed, blotting out the usual caution that would have me ensuring an easy dumping ground as well. Damn. If I was going to beat him up I would have needed to leave him alive to bruise and bleed. Damned scientific advances. I spot a boulder not far off, it is big enough to hide a body if I do some digging to give it a little space under the rock.

Walking over to look at it I see there is a great bed of leaves surrounding it, I work carefully to push the top layer back on one side so I can roll the rock over there while I prep the space beneath it. That done I roll it over and find a small den to one side. I'll have to be careful not to destroy that. I dig the space out as far away from the side with the den as possible and arrange the body in there to fit. I remember to search his pockets before I roll the rock back into place, removing a cell phone and his wallet. I roll the boulder back into place, fluffing what was crushed in its temporary place before I smooth the leaves back over it. Grabbing some branches I sweep the area, moving grasses and leaves around. Not the best but it will have to do.

I wonder if Jasmine is home?

Six

Mikael

The fire before me is warm and I resent needing it. I want my full vampire strength back. Damn that bitch for doing this to me. I can at least walk again. The time in bed was torture. Getting Vigo hired helped immensely, and he hired others for me to keep the house and to do my bidding in other matters. Pacing the room I go over what I will tell the council when I call them. I need to get this story just right, or they could decide to come after me. I know she is using her magic, at least some. Because she used it on me. The question is, do I tell them she used it on me or no? I think yes. I am incredibly weak and I can definitely play it up that I don't want to see her again for fear that she will hurt me again.

I will tell them she can walk in the sun as well, with my magic it will be easy enough to fake starting to burn if they decide to check me. I may use a glamour to appear more emaciated than I am, that could help to sway them to my cause. Decision made I walk over to my desk and pick up the phone, dialing the council number. The man that answers the phone on the fourth ring sounds bored as he says, "Council, state your business."

His tone irritates me but I swallow my annoyance, "Hello, this is Mikael Harris and I need to report a crime."

"Ooo, a crime? And what is the nature of the crime?"

The excitement he displays makes me wonder what he does all day, "The nature of the crime is a vampire with magic and the ability to walk in the sunlight."

The idiot on the other end screeches and drops the phone with a clatter. I don't know who he is fucking to have this job but I would like to strangle them both. He picks the phone up and I can hear him breathing heavily as he scratches out a note. "The next opening we have is two nights from now. Be here at eleven. The council will want any evidence you have to prove your accusations. I don't need to tell you it could go very badly for you if you were to make a false accusation, correct?"

"I am aware. I'll be there." I place the phone back in its cradle, leaning forward in my chair and steepling my hands. Vigo enters my office with a tray holding a decanter of blood and a wine glass. I watch as he pours and hands me the glass. Taking a sip I ask him, "Vigo, are you loyal to me?"

"Always sir. I am yours to do with as you will."

"Good. Good. I want you to do something, to prove your loyalty. And receive a gift at the same time."

"Yes sir, anything for you sir."

I unbutton the cuff of one sleeve before rolling it up. "I want you to drink from me here on my arm and then put a finger in the sunlight from this window." I use my magic to open the curtain just the smallest amount, it doesn't come easily. Sweat beads on my lip as it does finally move. It must be that I am still weak from being drained.

Vigo licks his lips, "Sir, are you sure? You are still healing from the great evil done to you. I don't want to slow the process with my feeding."

"It will be fine Vigo, do as I say." I hold my arm out and he falls to his knees before me, taking hold of my arm he is incredibly gentle as he brings his lips to my wrist. His teeth sink in and the pleasure travels up my arm to pool in my groin. He releases my wrist as I lean back into the chair.

"Sir, would you like help with, ahem, anything else?" His eyes drift down to my groin and I realize I have grown hard.

Unbuttoning my slacks I pull my cock out and point it toward him, he practically dives at it, wrapping his lips around it and swirling his tongue round the head. He circles the base with one hand to hold it in place as he sucks his way down my length. I groan with the pleasure of it as he withdraws while pressing his tongue against the underside. He sucks my cock better than anyone ever has, with his other hand snaking round to cup my ass. His nails pressing my ass he deep throats my cock hard and fast, all to soon my pleasure peaks and I am releasing deep in his throat as I hold the back of his head to keep myself buried to the hilt in his hot little mouth. I release him and he licks my cock clean before letting go. I fasten my pants as he wipes his mouth and licks his fingers clean, still on his knees before me.

"That was much nicer than I expected Vigo. Now, put a finger in the sunlight there."

He thrusts his finger into the sunlight with no hesitation and holds it there as it begins to burn. "Take the damn finger out of the sun Vigo!" He draws it away and waits for my next command. I take a long swig of the blood in my glass, it has cooled but it fills me still. "Move Vigo! How can it be that bitch is the only one I can pass my gift on to?" I thrust my hand into the light from the window to prove that I have it and my hand starts to smoke. I snatch it away, watching the redness fade as I use my magic to shut the curtain again. It is even more difficult this time but better than shutting it while I burn.

I down the rest of my glass as the rage rises within me. "How dare that bitch make me so weak that I am not even able to resist the sun! I made her!" I throw my glass, relishing the sound as it smashes against the fireplace. The rage courses through my body as I throw my chair and sweep my desk clean of everything resting on it. Vigo runs to a corner, cowering there. By the time the rage has subsided I have destroyed most of my office. I grab the decanter from the floor where it landed but somehow did not break and head for the door.

"Come Vigo. Get one of the maids to clean this mess. I have another job for you, meet me in my bedroom after you send someone to clean this."

Seven

Jasmine

The bookstore is crowded for a Wednesday night. I have the Uber let me out at the far end of the lot in a dark corner. I know they think it odd, but isn't like I have to worry about strange men hiding in the dark to do bad things to me now that I am the monster they should fear. And the last thing they will see if they get on my bad side. Walking into the store I wave at the witch behind the counter. She smiles and nods, letting me know that Helen is already back there waiting. I force myself to continue walking at a human pace. I am excited for the lessons and for getting better at controlling my magic so I don't overrun my house or room mates with anything else.

Slipping in the door at the back of the store I walk at a vampire pace down the hall to the room we meet in, tapping lightly on the door I let myself in and slow my walk. Helen doesn't freak out about how fast I am but she says it makes her dizzy. I set my bag on the floor next to my chair and sit down, Helen slides a strange tile toward me.

It is a large, square tile with designs and colors on each corner, a diamond in the middle has another design contained in the purple diamond. I see she also has a dusty tome off to one side that my fingers are itching to explore. "Ahem, Jasmine. Earth to Jasmine."

"Sorry, I was looking at your book. Are we going to get to look at it tonight?"

"Possibly, but first a test. I know we tested your magic before but I feel like it has grown since then. And definitely added new a dimension to your abilities. So we need to know just how many dimensions were added to your abilities. Put your hand over the fire corner." The look on my face must tell her I don't know which symbol is fire and she says, "The red one dear. The red one," her voice dry like autumn leaves.

Shrugging I hold my hand in the air above the red corner and flames lick across my hand. I snatch it away, only after realizing that it didn't hurt. Meeting Helen's eyes I see a twinkle in them as she holds back laughter. A wry twist to my own lips I put my hand back over the red corner and watch the flames rolling off my hand, turning it this way and that to see the effect.

"Now the blue please."

I move my hand across to the blue corner and water pours off it like a miniature waterfall though I feel no moisture on my hand.

"The green."

I move my hand to the green corner and fern-like leaves sprout from my skin. It is fascinating but if I lift my hand away to get a better look they fade into nothing. Her face looking pinched Helen tells me, "The white."

I move my hand to hover over that one and a small dust devil spins up from my hand. Tiny bits of dust and leaves float in the swirl.

All color drains from Helen's face as she says, "The purple."

Her voice is a bit choked and I ask, "Are you all right?"

She clears her throat, "I'm fine. Place your hand over the purple."

I do as she says and this beautiful translucent mist rises from my hand but I forget that as Helen wobbles like she will pass out, my chair goes flying as I jump out of it and race around the table to make sure she doesn't fall.

My hands on her shoulders I ask her, "Helen, what's wrong? Don't tell me you're fine because you obviously are not. What does this mean? Why are you so frightened?"

Helen recovers herself enough to look up at me and I see fear in her eyes for the first time. My heart sinks, I step back from her as she seems to be holding herself upright and the danger of her fainting is passed. "The test. It fits. It all fits, oh shit, oh shit, not this one. Why now? Oh shit, oh shit."

I reach down and give her a little shake, "Helen! What are you talking about? You're making no sense!"

She stands and starts to pace the room, walking the length of the table before turning to walk it again. All the while she mumbles, "I'm not good enough for this. I don't have enough experience, I can't teach her all she needs to know."

I watch her as she paces, just staying out of the way. Suddenly she stops and starts shouting at the ceiling, "What were you thinking? She needs someone stronger than me!"

A dark woman appears in the middle of the room, I don't know who she is but I can feel the power, the danger, rolling off her like too much perfume. I grab Helen and thrust her behind me, taking a defensive stance before her. I feel Helen peering around me and I shove her further behind me. Behind me she exclaims, "Holy fuck-sticks! Get down Jasmine!" Then she moves over next to me and prostrates herself, tugging on my arm, still telling me, "Down! Dammit Jasmine, kneel!"

I whisper to her, "No! This woman is dangerous! I'm protecting you!"

The lady before me starts laughing. Her laugh is loud and harsh, she says, "Oh child, this is why I chose you." She wipes tears from her eyes, "You don't even know who you offer to fight and yet you stand before the woman next to you ready to fight to the death for her."

* * *

Helen straightens enough to look at the woman, "Please forgive her, she doesn't know. She doesn't recognize you. She didn't know anything about our world a month ago. She is barely trained. She needs someone better to train her. I am not enough for training her. She needs better than me. Please forgive—"

The woman laughs again, "Get up Helen, have a seat in your chair. Jasmine, help her up. Mortal knees are not sturdy and she is older."

I am confused as I help Helen to her feet, but it would seem murder isn't on the menu. The woman walks over and creates her own chair out of thin air. I help Helen get seated and I take my own seat next to her.

The woman across from us speaks, "Hello Jasmine, most call me Hekate though there are some that call me by other names. Helen already knows of me, though I am not one of her patron gods. Helen, you were chosen just as much as Jasmine was, you are exactly who she needs to train her. The copy of the prophecy you have is... incomplete." She waves her hand and thick scroll appears on the table before us. "This is a complete and unedited version of the prophecy, it should relieve some worries. Your gods knew this was coming, they'll be speaking to you more directly from now on."

"Oh fuck, oh fuck, oh fuck…" Helen puts her head in her hands, her oh fucks devolving into indistinguishable mumbles.

Hekate scowls, snapping her fingers at Helen she says, "Get yourself together!"

Helen looks up at her, "If what I have read isn't even the entire prophecy, oh sweet Gods, how bad will it get?"

Hekate scoffs, "Baahh! What you read was mangled garbage! It was all butchered by men determined that men and money would be the savior of the this world. They were certain they could alter the words of the prophecy and change the way things happen. That didn't work so they just cut out large chunks of it, making it a prophecy of doom. Read the full and accurate prophecy, it won't be an easy journey." She looks over to me, "The chosen one here is going to be a giant pain in the ass."

Helen goes back to mumbling, her head in her hands. Three more strangers appear in the room, Hekate isn't concerned so I wait to see what they do. They look from Helen to Hekate and scowl. One of them snaps, "Why must you frighten her like this?"

They lift her and bundle her off to the other side of the room, leaving me with Hekate. She smiles at me, it is less comforting than I think she intends it to be. I think she must realize this as she dispenses with the smile, telling me, "Ask your questions. I will answer what I can."

Looking over at the new strangers that appear to be comforting Helen my first question has to be, "Who are they? Does Helen know them? Is she safe?"

Hekate shakes her head, chuckling, "Those are her

patrons. They are Hermes, Brighid, and Hera. Your friend is safer with them than she is even with you. Now that you are reassured of her safety, are there questions you would like to ask that relate to the matter at hand?"

I nod, "May I have a copy of the prophecy too?" She waves a hand, a second copy appears next to the first. "I, um, am I going to destroy the world?"

"You could, if you really wanted to do it. But part of the reason why I chose to nudge you into the space of chosen is your heart and sense of justice. You personally, in most of your lives have experienced grave injustices. Some due to society, some visited upon you by that idiot you were wed to in your first life, and still others by virtue of the family you were born into. All of those injustices created the soul within you that rejects those behaviors. You can no more visit injustice upon the world than you could murder Helen there for your own hunger. That is why when you went hunting for the first time you insisted on it being a person that hurt people. A drug dealer that preyed upon children and the weak."

My eyes grow round, "How did you know about that?"

"The same way I know about most things you do, I keep a watch on you. You are important to me and to the rest of the world."

"Why? Why all this? Why a prophecy? You are a goddess, aren't you omnipotent? What do you need me for?"

Hekate sighs, "Of course you would ask this question. It is so much easier to deal with a hero. They never ask insightful questions. It's always, point me at the bad guy so I can smash. Less delicate maneuvers but also none of the hard questions. The short answer is no, we are not omnipotent. We also don't get to decide the order of the universe. We are much more powerful than even the most powerful magical being. The downside to that is that we are bound by more rules. I won't get into all the rules with you, I assure you they are mostly boring and simply ensure that we cannot take away free will of anyone nor can we alter the timeline in a substantial manner. We can nudge things, little pushes to the order of things to help it go the way that provides what we see as the best possible outcome. The problem is, some of us would prefer a different sort of order. One that is all about control and power. They also can make little pushes, nudge people and events to bring about the kind of order they prefer. I, we, need you to right things that we didn't prevent many years ago."

"Things? What kind of things?"

She looks away, "The society we have now, one built upon greed and power. It was never meant to be like this. It is a perversion of what was meant to be. Our time to make the necessary corrections is growing short. You, are the only one that had a life thread that could be nudged into the right place. The only one. No others were suitable for this. If you fail, we all fail."

"Great. No pressure. What do I need to do? How do I fix this?"

"The long and short of it is that you need to be you. Continue to make the decisions that honor your heart. I have great faith in the person you have become, you are not one to go along to make things easier for yourself or anyone else. You go where your heart leads you and it will never lead you wrong."

"I don't mean to seem ungrateful here, but that isn't real specific. And as for my heart not leading me astray, you've been watching all this time. My heart has definitely led me astray. The two I would point out here for most recent fuck-ups are my departed husband Fabio and Mikael. I didn't end up in a whole relationship with Mikael this time but I missed all the signals that could have told me he was going to try to murder me."

She laughs, "Ah, but that wasn't your heart. Those things were your mind. Your mind told you that you should be fair. Or in the case of Fabio, your mind knew that your heart wouldn't let you use him to get you out of your aunt's home. So it told you that you must love him. Because it was only okay in your mind if you left with him because you loved him. As for Mikael, you felt you owed him for 'saving' you. However, the reality is that he did you a disservice. Had you gone with Leonidas he would have turned you that very night. You wouldn't have had to convince anyone to do it and you likely would have had sex very soon after that. But, fear is a magical motivator, more often than not in the wrong direction."

"It would seem that way." I look away. Leonidas would have turned me that night? I thought for sure he was going to kill me. "So I was supposed to go with him that night? That was what was supposed to happen?"

"It was what we hoped would happen. As for what is supposed to happen, well there is no such thing. The order of things is ever changing ordered chaos."

"What? Well that is fucking annoying. So there is no certain way things are supposed to be? The universe is just running around all crazy and doing what it wants?"

"Yes and no. The universe is vast and beyond even the scope of the gods to understand it all. There are those that came before us, they tend to the order of all things. We just try to nudge things toward what we can see as the best possibility. We can see some of the patterns over time. Seers can often get glimpses of the bigger picture and we tend to work around those. They are wildly frustrating with the way they are often vague and sometimes entire sections are just intentionally unintelligible until certain things have happened."

"Oh fuck, that's even worse. Is this one," I gesture at the copy she provided for me, "one of the ones that has the intentionally unintelligible sections?"

She smirks at me, "What do you think?"

"I think getting out of bed was just asking for it today."

Eight

Leonidas

The first jobsite I have chosen has only a single road into what will eventually be a neighborhood with a cul de sac at the far end. For now I have a parcel marked as the start project. This one will be our model home, it will also be on the smallest lot. As I pull up to the lot I see a couple cars I recognize and more vampires that chose to walk here. Getting out of my truck I call everyone over.

Once they are gathered I begin, "I am happy to see you all here. It means a lot to me that you are choosing to be part of this change from gang into family. As we make these changes, we are stepping out of the drug business and into the home business. With our strength and speed, with no audience we can complete things in half the time a normal company would. That being said, we still need to protect our secret. We are going to build the entire neighborhood up, but none of the finishing materials will be installed until someone buys the home. When the house is bought they will choose their materials and we will install them overnight. There will be a privacy fence around each of the home sites. Part of our brand will be that each home is privacy fenced, to make good neighbors. This will also help to protect us from being seen moving faster than any human can move. We will all take turns patrolling the area, to ensure that no one gets close enough to see. Is everyone with me so far?"

I watch the crowd as they nod and shuffle around a bit.

"Good. Now for the part you may not appreciate. We will be working with shifters. Wolves mostly. But they have been working for me for a long time. They know the house building business and though they have spent a long time working at staying the same speed as everyone else, they are capable of working just as quickly as we do." I hear the sound of an engine coming this way even as the groans begin. "Speaking of, here they come. I know you don't have a lot of experience with them but you need to put forth the effort. They are just the same as all of you, trying to get by in a world that doesn't want to know we exist."

"Don't shifters eat vampires?" Linus asks.

I shake my head but before I can answer Banner says, "Only when they invite us to eat them. I haven't had any complaints."

Mila laughs, "I haven't tried shifter before, maybe I need to add some variety to my diet."

Banner tells her, "I invite you to test the theory at your earliest convenience."

"Moving on," I wave my shifter crew round to stand in front of me, "this crew has a lot more experience than any of you have in building houses. They will be training you, being nice to them means your training will go that much smoother.

Nine

Jasmine

The book store is crowded tonight. It is odd slipping through them, unnoticed. Helen explained to me that when the place started to attract more of the magical community a few of the witches got together and put a don't see us spell on the place. It isn't really meant to make the magical community invisible and if a satyr walked the aisles in their natural form I think someone might notice. It does in general keep human eyes on themselves and other humans.

The hallway is cool and quiet, Helen is waiting in the room for me. Opening the door I can tell she is doing so much better than last time I saw her. Her scent is not like last time, it's happier and stronger.

"Hello Jasmine! I have been reading the original of the prophecy and it is so much better for the planet as a whole. Fascinating how they left in the wording to identify the chosen one but made everything they would do seem to be a tragedy for the world. Guess we know what kind of people did the edits there, eh? Come, sit."

I sit in the chair across from her, as she starts to explain what she has read in the prophecy so far. She is listing off all these great things I am supposed to cause in some way and my ears start to ring. I can't hear what she is saying anymore and all I can think is how am I going to do this? I couldn't even save myself from a bad marriage? How am I going to save the world? This isn't me, they must have the wrong person. The room starts to spin and then Helen is in front of me, her warm hands on my face. Sound slowly returns and I hear her asking if I'm okay. My eyes burn, my vision blurs. "I can't. You have the wrong person. It can't be me. I can't do all that! I couldn't even save myself, how can I save the world? I'm just nobody." Helen's hands drop from my face as I stand too quickly, the chair flying back. "I have to go. I can't do this. I just need to go, stop wasting your time. I can't keep the whole world safe, I don't even know if I can keep the few that are family safe. What if I fuck it up worse? I need to go."

I run out, the sound of her calling my name fading away behind me as I slip through the book store unseen by eyes that can't track a vampire moving at speed.

* * *

Helen

I call after Jasmine but she is gone before the her name echoes through the room. Walking over to the table I pick up my phone. Jasmine isn't in a good place right now. Maybe I didn't handle this right? I am too old for this shit. I tap the screen a few times and bring up Scarlett's number. The call barely rings through and she answers it, "Hello?"

"Hi Scarlett, this is Helen. You remember me?"

"Yes, Jasmine's witch teacher."

"Yes. The witch teacher." I say wryly, "So Jasmine just ran out like her tail is on fire. Do you have any idea where she would go when she is upset?"

"Upset? Why is she upset? What did you do?"

"I didn't do anything. She got here and I was talking to her about the prophecy. Next thing I know, she is zoned out and paler than usual. I got her attention but then she started going off about not being the one, about not being able to do this and then she ran out."

"Oh no. I don't actually know where she would go. Vampires tend to be more secretive than most. Jasmine is still new but she has had it rough. I don't know... I can ask around. Maybe Chloe knows something? Or Leonidas? I will check with them. One of us will let you know if we hear from her, you'll do the same for us, right?"

"Of course. Thank you. Tell her I am here to listen too, not just teach. Or I will when I see her again."

* * *

Scarlett

Helen hangs up on her end and Chloe walks into the room, "I heard some of that. Jasmine is missing?"

I shrug, "Sort of? I mean, she hasn't been gone long but she ran out upset. I am going to call Quinn, see if he has any idea. Will you call Eason?"

She nods as she pulls out her phone. The call with Quinn

is quick, he hasn't seen her since she dumped Mikael into the front hall of Morhall. I call Sebastian next, he hasn't seen her but says he will check the downtown area and see if he can sniff her out there. Chloe finishes a call with Asher and shrugs, she hasn't got anything either.

I call Leonidas' company and tell them to have him call me now, it's about Jasmine. I don't have his personal number, it has never been something I needed before now. Five minutes of pacing later my phone rings, "Hello?"

"Scarlett? This is Leonidas. What's wrong with Jasmine?"

"She went to her lesson tonight and her teacher called not long after to tell us she had run out upset. Do you have any idea where she might have gone?"

"What is she upset about? She doesn't usually run from anything."

"Helen said she was talking to her about some prophecy?"

"Oh. You know, I have an idea. I need to go check on it. Is this your cell?"

"It is."

"I'll text you if I find her. Give me thirty, forty minutes."

He ends the call with that and I look at Chloe, "We might have a lead."

She walks over to wrap her arms around my shoulders, "Don't worry, she's a survivor and stronger than she thinks she is. She'll be ok and come back fine. She just needs a little time is all. She never had people worry about her before, it probably hasn't occurred to her that we would worry."

* * *

Leonidas

. . .

Pointing my truck at the observatory I gun it. I don't know for sure that she will go there, but it seemed to comfort her when I brought her last time and she had just gotten a prophecy from my mom that night.

Twenty minutes later I arrive and park the truck. Stepping in the door I find the usual door guy and ask him, "Did the lady I brought here not long ago come in tonight by any chance?"

"She did. She's in there now but she looks real sad tonight. You two have a fight?"

I shake my head no, "She has much bigger problems than me friend. Thanks," I dig a twenty out of my wallet, "here, any time she comes in, just put her on my account."

He nods and waves me on through. I set the bill on his podium as I pass by him, the lights slowly dimming as I near the door at the other end. I shoot off a quick text, letting Scarlett know I found her and I will bring her home eventually. Opening the door as quietly as possible and slipping in to close it behind me, I spot her immediately. She is on the far side of the theater, sitting well away from everyone. There is a man sitting well behind her looking at her like she might be his next meal. He smells like he doesn't wash and if he bothers her, well, the world will just be better off when she eliminates him. Reaching her side I ask in a whisper no one else could hear, "Is this seat taken?"

She smiles sadly at me, waving at the seat to let me know I can sit with her. I learned early on in life that sitting with a woman who is not interested in your company can be very dangerous to your person, and I have always assumed that the danger would be that much greater with a woman that is also a vampire. "Want to talk about it?"

She whispers to me, "I went to my lesson today and Helen was in a much better state, that was great. Then she started telling me about the prophecy and all these things I am supposed to do, things that are supposed to save the world. None of it sounded like me. What if I fuck it all up? The world isn't great right now, but it isn't completely fucked either. What if I fuck things up so bad they can't be fixed? Who thought it was a good idea to put me in charge of saving anything? I couldn't even save myself! You and your gang accidentally saved me when you killed him."

I didn't realize her situation when she was human was so bad. She never talked about it, but I thought that was just because it was her human life. "I don't know much about the life you had as a human. The little I know about you since I have met you tells me that you were not simply waiting to be saved. What we did may have hurried the process of you being able to get away from whatever that situation was, but I have no doubt that you would have made it out without us. As for this, you aren't alone. I don't think you would fuck it up anyway because you care. You care entirely too much to fuck it up. You wouldn't be sitting here worried about it if you were the kind that would destroy the world by accident. And, like I said, you have friends to help you."

"But how can I involve my friends knowing that my choices could kill them all? "

"How could you not involve us knowing your choices are life or death for us? They and I do not want you to carry this alone. You are not alone in this, you have all of us. Every one of us would do a great many things for you."

"Are you sure? I feel like this is so much to ask of anyone."

"I feel very sure that we would all be offended if you don't let us help you."

She shrugs, "I guess. I just have a hard time relying on anyone. Historically it hasn't worked out so well. Were you sent to bring me back?"

"Sort of. I was asked if I had an idea where you might be. I messaged them that I found you and would bring you back later."

"Do you mind if we finish the show before we go?"

"I wouldn't have it any other way." I tell her as I slip my arm around her shoulders.

She snuggles in and sighs, "How did you know I would be here anyway?"

"It was a guess. This was where I brought you the night we got that prophecy from my mom, you seemed to take comfort being here. I thought it was worth a try to check this place first."

Ten

Mikael

The council has me waiting like a common petitioner. It's an outrage, and a ridiculous show of power. There are no other petitioners and the business they tend to is so little as to be laughable. It's fine, I will play their games and they will do my bidding whether they realize it or not. Vigo sits in one of the chairs while I pace. My left leg is damnably stiff, it hasn't finished healing still. I can't believe that bitch was so lucky.

At least the visible injury will help to sway them to my plans. The door opens and I look up as the lackey asks us to follow him. He leads us into the council chamber and closes the door behind us as he leaves the room. No chairs, so this is to be a standing testimony. Great.

Brian says, "What crime is it that you must report Mikael?"

"I need to report a crime acted upon my person."

Bianca sighs loudly, "We do not police personal fights between vampires Mikael. Is that all you have?"

"No, the attack is only the vehicle for how I found out the crimes concealed. If it please the council I will explain."

Rick nods, "Go ahead and tell your story. We will decide if there is a crime to concern us."

"Recently a woman seemed to find me and she immediately begged my aid to save her life from a gang of vampires that had been feeding in the area. I felt drawn to her. I couldn't leave her in the hands of the brutes. I took her home with me. It was a mistake, but as I said, I felt drawn to her. She knew our nature before she asked for aid and soon after I brought her home she became very insistent that I turn her, to solve all her problems. I was resistant to the idea. She seduced me and I turned her in a fit of lust. Once turned she quickly left my home and wanted little to do with me. One evening I went to her abode, where she seduced me and then attacked me viciously. During the attack she used magic to blast me through a wall, into a tree where my spine was broken in several places. Before I could recover from that she drained me, leaving me too weak to heal properly. The injuries from that attack are why I limp now.

It was nearing daylight and I thought for sure I would die. She rolled me up in a rug and carried me off to leave me to die in a dumpster. It was full daylight when she dumped me there and left."

The room erupts into discussion of how these things could be and whether or not I could be lying. When they decide to question me further all faces turn toward me and Tiara speaks.

"What proof do you have of this?"

"I have the blanket she wrapped me in for transport. I can give you the address to find the tree I was blasted into. Also, Vigo here," I gesture toward him and he steps forward, "is the one I called to help me from where she dumped me."

Vigo cowers as they look him over and Tiara asks, "When did he call you?"

"It was early morning when he called. We were both quite concerned as he had to stay there the entire day and there was a possibility that humans could find him or that the dumpster was slated for emptying that day. Either would have created a host of problems."Felicity shares a look with Tiara. They still seem skeptical as Felicity says, "So you stayed in the dumpster the entire day? And this," she gestures to Vigo, "one came to get you after nightfall. How have you healed? As for time of day, you were grievously injured, it is possible you are mistaken about the time of day. Why should we believe this is anything other than a lover's quarrel? It is not unknown for a witch to become a vampire. It isn't ideal but, thus far it has not been any great tragedy. They stand to lose as much as we do if the humans find out about them."

Fucking annoying bitch asking all these damn questions. "I understand why you would ask that and I feel it my duty to tell you that she is one of a group of witches that plan a rise to power. They only needed one to become vampire. They have created a spell that allows them to walk in the day light, which she is already utilizing. They don't intend to stop with just us, they want the world. She made a call while she was taking me to the dumpster. I think she didn't realize I was still conscious. I heard them talking about who she would turn and how their plans were progressing. They are planning to take over the world and they are starting with us."

Brian leans forward, "Putting aside the question of world domination, since your only proof in that matter is that you overheard a phone call, how have you healed so quickly? If your injuries were that dire, how are you able to stand before us now?"

"Sheer force of will. I am still healing and have had to

drink copious amounts of blood to even be able to regain the ability to stand. Walking is a recent achievement. It pains me to admit that I still have a limp as I am not fully healed."

I watch as the council exchanges looks before Bianca tells me I may go wait in the common area while they discuss my case. I leave feeling hopeful and exaggerating my limp.

* * *

Mikael

It seems like they take days before they leave the council room. I entered the common room to find there were several other petitioners already in there waiting. They must have saved the most difficult case for last and I agree with that decision, it is what I would have done. Solve all the petty cases before tackling the one that requires more thought and consideration before acting.

I avoid mingling with the others in here, they are obviously beneath me. The wait is ended as double doors at the far end of the room open before the council members. Refreshments are brought in and they begin to mingle with those that have been waiting. Scott heads my way and I wait patiently for him while Vigo brings me a drink.

"We discussed your report Mikael. We will need to do some investigation of our own before we are willing to think about calling her in to question."

"What? That's outrageous! Why isn't she being dragged in by the hair right now?"

Scott sighs and rubs the bridge of his nose with one hand, "I have got to stop betting against Felicity. Look, we don't do that without a lot of good evidence. You don't have that. All you have is a story that is, well, less than plausible. We have good relations with the witches, they may not have a specific council but they do have leaders and we talk. They are not looking to rule the world. There may be some rogue witches that do want that but most of them want to talk to their plants and their animals. Get together and drink tea while they research things. World domination doesn't leave much time for any of that. You would know that if you studied the world around you. So, while we are going to check into your claims, do not expect much to come of it."

Vigo hands me a red wine fortified with blood. "I understand. Perhaps she is one of the rogue witches. Or maybe they have fostered a relationship with you to present that image while working behind the scenes to achieve their actual goal. I feel confident that council investigations will uncover anything untoward."

"Untoward? Jeez man, you need to get out more. Your verbiage reveals you to be older than you appear. Or have you stopped being around humans entirely?"

"I do entertain humans occasionally, but mostly at charity events and such. Their manner of speaking changes slower and that suits me, I don't like much of the newer language. Yeeting something baffles me."

Scott laughs, "Well old man, I personally enjoy yeeting people and things as needed. People especially."

I sip my drink, I have no idea what yeeting means and I can't tell what my reaction should be. I end up finishing my drink in one go and realize that I am thirsty again, "Vigo, please get me another." I turn back to Scott, "I am afraid I must leave earlier than I had planned. It is rare to get the opportunity to mingle with the council and I was looking forward to getting to know more of you, but my injuries still have me weak as a kitten. I must go home, rest and feed. It seems to be all I do these days."

Scott claps my shoulder and I stumble, a little more than needed. He catches me before I hit the ground, "Dammit man, I didn't realize you were injured so deeply. You really are quite weak still, aren't you?"

I straighten painfully, "I dislike admitting it, but yes. Walking is still difficult and the hearing with all the standing was taxing on reserves I don't have right now."

Scott's lips press together and his brow draws down, "I am sorry I didn't realize. Would you like an escort home?"

"Thank you, no. I have Vigo to help me in," I say right as Vigo appears with the next drink, straight blood this time. "Once I get home I will feed and rest."

He nods and steps back, "Rest well old man. We will be thorough in our investigation."

I limp out, Vigo at my side ready to help me should I falter. I keep my smile on the inside as the investigation that would have been lackluster at best will now be a much more thorough one. I can only hope they catch her doing magic or walking in the sunlight.

Eleven

Jasmine

Leonidas sat with me for the rest of the show before escorting me out to his truck. It is getting close to morning, if he comes in he will need to stay with us today in order to keep the secret of our day walking. As he pulls into the drive I ask, "Would you like to come in?"

He looks at the sky, "Are you sure?"

"I am. I think I would like the company today."

He nods and puts the truck in park, shutting it off as we both open our doors. He appears at my side as I start for the house and I take his hand in mine. I have always been amazed at how something so simple as a hand to hold when you feel shaky can make such a difference. Entering the house I hear Scarlett and Chloe in the living area, knowing I have some explaining to do we head that way.

Scarlett looks me over as I enter and Chloe asks, "Are you feeling better now?"

Nodding I say, "Yes. Mostly."

Scarlett huffs, "Great, now sit your ass down and tell us why you ran off and scared poor Helen half to death."

We sit on one of the couches and I kick my shoes off to pull my feet up on the couch and wrap my arms around my knees. "It was just to much. Helen was telling me all these great things I am supposed to do, things I can't imagine how I could be trusted with the responsibility of, and I spiraled."

Leonidas rubs my shoulders with one hand, a comfort I lean into. Chloe says, "You were afraid because you think you can't handle the responsibility?"

"Yes, and no. I mean, I can handle responsibility but for the world? That's so much. And they want me to save the world? Save it? I couldn't even save myself from a bad marriage without help."

Scarlett laughs, "Oh girl, you don't have to do anything alone. We got you."

"I didn't want to possibly put either of you in danger. You two, or Leonidas here, or any of the guys. All of you have been better to me than anyone in my life since my parents died. The idea of risking losing you... it just terrifies me." I wipe at my eyes, blood tears betraying the deep emotions roiling inside me.

Leonidas pulls me close, letting me rest on him.

Chloe nods, "I think we can understand that. We each have our own stories of loss from before we became vampires. But Scarlett and I have had more time to adjust. We have each of us been around for a long time, and more than a few lives before the one the ended in being a vampire. So, you get a pass this time. But, we need you to lean on us and trust us. You are our friend and we will help you any way we can."

Sniffling a little I tell her, "I'll do my best." I see a ray of light peeking through one of the heavy curtains, "Hey, since it is well past daybreak now, want to see me in the sunlight?"

Scarlett laughs, "Nice subject change but yes."

I point at the window that has the sunlight peeking through, "We will go over there and open that curtain. Maybe you two go over to the other side of the room?"

We all get in place and the Leonidas and I slowly pull the curtains open and step into the light. It is warm on my back and feels nice. I notice Leonidas taking off his jacket and stretching in the sunlight. His jacket hides a lot of his build and those arms are thick. I could watch him stretch in the sunlight for a hot minute.

"Holy shit, it's true. You really can stand in the sunlight without burning up." Chloe says while clutching Scarlett's hand. They both walk around to get near the sun and hold a finger out to be sure it is sunlight. Their fingers start to smoke as they enter the light from the window and they yank them away, stepping back as well. I take that as my cue and turn to shut the curtains. Leonidas draws the other side this way and our hands meet in the middle. It feels like small sparks pass between our hands and suddenly all I want to do is get him upstairs. But first, a little extra protection for my friends.

Turning back toward Chloe and Scarlett I find them standing barely a foot away from me. Both look incredibly excited. Scarlett asks, "So how does this go?"

"Well, I would like to see if it is possible for someone that got it from me to pass it on. My idea is that one of you drinks from me and the other from Leonidas. We test the theory the same way that you did a minute ago, we will open the curtain and you stick a finger toward the light. Are you both up for that?"

Chloe shakes her head emphatically, "Hell yes we are. Scarlett, you get her because I know you want to, I'll give Leonidas a taste test."

Chloe steps over to Leonidas who offers an arm while Scarlett walks around her to get closer to me. Never one to pass up an opportunity I flip my hair back off my shoulder and tip my head, offering her my favorite spot. She leans in close, her hands drifting up to caress my arms as she inhales my scent before her lips press that sweet spot so gently. Her lips open, never breaking contact with my skin and her tongue darts down for a lick. Teeth meet skin and the exquisite pleasure pain of her bite begins. A shiver runs through my body and straight to my core, melting me. All too soon she releases me from the ecstasy of her bite. Her hands remain on my arms as she steps back and I am grateful as I feel her steady me when I instinctively sway toward her.

Chloe clears her throat and I open my eyes. She looks flushed and so does Leonidas. I imagine I do too as I look toward Scarlett. She is licking her lips, her gaze a promise of another time and place very soon. Chloe says, "Um, you two maybe need some time alone? It's getting warm in here and vampire sweat is not pretty."

I clear my throat as Scarletts hands drop from my arms, "I guess we need to see if it worked. You two step back and we will open the curtains."

They step back, probably farther than necessary. Opening the curtains we step back to wait. Chloe goes first, a single finger reaching for the light but starting to smoke and drawn back so much faster. Scarlett reaches one hand toward the light, all her fingers extended. They slip into the light, her dark skin seeming to soak in the rays and come to brilliant life. She steps fully into the sunlight, arms outstretched and feet apart, her face tipped up to feel the rays. A sigh of contentment escapes her lush lips. Chloe watches, her lips parted and the fingers of one hand twitching toward the sun. I walk behind Scarlett to reach Chloe and offer her the same spot Scarlett so recently drank from but the other side. Chloe isn't slow or sweet, she pulls me to her, pinning my body against hers as she lowers her mouth to my neck. She bites hard and my core clenches, slickness spilling onto my panties. She drinks deeply, and releases my neck almost as quickly but holds me pinned to her while I collect myself.

Leonidas sounds strained as he says, "The temperature in here goes up a couple degrees every time someone bites you. I can't tell if it is just hot watching your reaction or if maybe your magic is leaking in a new way."

Chloe steps back, holding to my shoulders in case I sway. I smile at her, "Go on, give it a try now." I turn to watch her step into the sun her pale skin seeming to glow in the sun as her eyes drift closed and blood tears slip down her face. I do a brief check on my magic and I am not leaking this time. I slip behind the two soaking up the sun and put an arm around Leonidas.

He murmurs, "They might stand there the entire day."

Chuckling I say, "I think they have earned it. I have more pressing concerns now though, I need to feed. I think we have some blood in the fridge. You staying here to watch the sun worship or would you like a drink as well?"

"I'd like a drink. I feel a little parched, I didn't feed last night and Chloe is voracious."

"Ha, yes, I noticed," I say as we start for the kitchen.

"I noticed you noticing, the scent of your desire was intoxicating."

I feel his arm snake around my waist, the world spins and I am pressed against a wall in the kitchen, his body hard against mine as he whispers next to my ear, "I need you. To bury myself inside you while you moan at the pleasure I give you. Eat fast."

My entire body shivers with anticipation as he steps back. A deep breath and I head for the fridge, my core throbbing. I hear him inhale deeply as grab a couple bags of blood. I turn and he looks predatory. I feel a surge of excitement in my chest. His teeth have descended and I walk over to him stopping inches away, raising one of the bags between us. He takes it from me with a growl. I smile and bring my own to my lips, puncturing the bag with my teeth before I retract them and suck the bag dry. Tossing it toward the trash I look up at him still drinking from his own and grin. His eyes narrow and I take off running. I am at the upstairs landing by the time he explodes out of the kitchen and stops to scent the air. I wait for him to see me, grin and wave as I take off for my room. Inside my room I stop an face the door, arms outstretched to either side as he barrels in, slamming me against his body. I wrap my arms around him as he lifts me up and buries his face in my chest. His hand slips between us and rips my shirt down the front. Shoving the material out of the way he pulls the cup of my bra, tugging it below my breast.

He latches on to my nipple and sucks hard, I moan with the pleasure of it. Then he nibbles it and I feel my panties get soaked. He releases my nipple, inhales and sets me down, his hands going to my pants. I bat them away and tell him, "Take care of your own clothes," when he growls at me.

He makes quick work of his clothing, kicking his boots off while snatching his shirt over his head. I remove all my clothing and my shoes just as quickly, the instant my panties hit the floor he lifts me up into his arms and crosses to the bed. I see the door standing open and send a little magic to close it as he lays me down on the bed.

He stands there just staring down at me, this intense look on his face and I ask, "Is there something wrong?"

His mouth lifts on one side in a half smile, "I just like to admire my meal for a moment before I feast." He leans down, hands going to my knees, spreading them slowly as he presses kisses to the inside of each thigh. When he reaches my pussy he kisses it softly at first, then his tongue slips in to swirl and stroke and my eyes roll back in my head. His tongue works its way up to my clit and a thumb enters me, giving my core something to clench around. Between the suction of his mouth and the magic of his tongue I cum on his face quickly, the spasms of my body rocking me on his thumb and sending further waves of pleasure reverberating through me.

His beautiful mouth pulls away from me as he straightens and pulls me to the edge of the bed. He could pull me straight to hell and I wouldn't care right now. I watch as he takes his large cock in his hand and rubs it along my soaking slit, causing me to convulse when he presses it on my clit. With a grin he slides it down and lines up with my core, just pressing most of the head in he grabs my thighs and pushes in slowly, his hands gripping my thighs so hard I would bruise if I were human. The feeling of my pussy stretching around his cock is amazing and watching the painful pleasure crossing his face as he forces himself to go slow makes it even hotter.

When he is buried fully in me I rock my hips quickly down and back up, his nails dig into my thighs as he sucks air. His eyes open and he pulls back till only the head is left in, he slams back into me and rails me with a ferocity that sends me soaring back toward an explosion. My eyes roll back and I grip the bed, then he shifts his hips and he is hitting my clit with every thrust. I explode in a million pieces as he slams into me and stays pressed against me as he flies over his own cliff.

Our breathing still ragged he lets go of my thighs, planting his hands on the bed on either side of me. Taking a full breath I say, "Want to spend the day with me?"

He pants, "I thought you'd never ask."

Twelve

Mikael

The report from the people I have watching Jasmine was mostly useless. I know where she goes most of the time but I don't know anything about her plans or what she does where she goes. Like the bookshop. She almost never comes out with books but she goes there at least weekly. I need to know why.

I know what I need to do, I just dread calling her. But having someone on the inside of Leonidas' group will provide me with plenty of information about her movements. She is obviously with him now, if I have someone in his gang listen to their conversations and maybe drive a wedge between them. Perhaps if she is completely broken by betrayal she will come back to me.

Yes. That could work. Picking up my phone and scrolling to her number, I call Daphne.

"Hello?"

"Daphne, hello. I'm sure you never expected I would call you but I have a job I think you might be interested in."

"Oh really? What's the pay like?"

"That depends on you. A thousand every time you pass me useful information, nothing if it doesn't tell me more about what I want to know. Are you interested?"

"I am. Money talks to me in a very personal way. What or should I say who, do you want to know about?"

"Jasmine. And by extension Leonidas as relates to her."

"Hmm, well, I think I can get back in with the gang easily enough. He restructured the gang and decided they would all be a family and go legit. That Jasmine chick is a bad influence on him. Everything was fine before she came along."

"Ah, do I detect a note of jealousy?"

"Maybe. I was angling for him before he found her and you ran off with her. After that night, he wouldn't look twice at me."

"Well, there is a large bonus in it for you if you can drive a wedge between them. You and I could both benefit from that, though you would benefit more than I."

"How big a bonus are we talking?"

"One million if she hates him for betraying her. Half that if they just break up."

"I'm your girl."

"Excellent. But, stay far away from Jasmine, she is so much more dangerous than anyone realizes."

"That cupcake? You must be kidding."

"Not at all. Don't be fooled by her looks, she is a vicious con artist and a killer witch. I have reported her to the council but they just don't seem to realize the gravity of the situation."

"A witch you say? Like casting spells and stuff?"

"Yes. Only her spells will hold you immobile while she drains you completely, taking your essence and absorbing some of your power, leaving you weak as a kitten while she dumps your body somewhere to fry in the sunlight."

"What? Holy fuck. Is that what happened to you? I heard you were laid up for a while, it seemed weird for a vampire to be laid up."

"It is. I am lucky to have good friends that would come save me."

"Shit. I don't want her killing Leonidas. Ok. You got a deal. I'll go get back in the gang. One sob story and he will melt. I'll call you soon."

She ends the call and I smile. It was so much easier to convince her than I thought it would be. I am finally strong enough that I can have a drink without needing it to be fortified with blood and I think a celebration is in order. The liquor cabinet in my office is well stocked, Vigo is proving to be the best assistant I have ever had. I select a well aged scotch and pour myself a three finger glassful. The first sip is magnificent. I take my drink with me to sit in my chair like an old man, the healing is slow. So slow. Damned woman! Why couldn't she just die?

Thirteen

Jasmine

I wake up in Leonidas' arms and it's nice. I was married for years and it never felt so nice as this to wake up next to him. I feel him stirring next to me and I sit up. I still feel like I need space sometimes, like I'll get trapped in another bad relationship. The money still doesn't seem real most of the time. Come to think of it, I should buy a car. I can get around just fine without it but having it would make it easier to avoid being seen by other vampires or their watchers if I go out in the daytime.

Leonidas gets out of the bed and stretches, I turn to watch the show. He pads off to the bathroom and I get out of the bed to dress. It's probably still hot as hell outside and I think I am going to go hunting tonight. Digging through the pile of clothing in my closet I find a mini skort made of stretchy fabric and half a shirt. Slipping all that on I pick out my shoes for today, heeled combat style boots. What is taking him so long in the bathroom? Water starts running and I realize he is getting a shower. Well shit. I was planning to do that as soon as I got him going. Oh well, I'll get one later. It isn't like I am going to smell anyway.

I head downstairs with my phone in hand, looking for dealerships open later. I find one and give them a call. Two minutes of talking to a salesperson and I have a ten o'clock appointment.

Meandering my way through the house I make my way to the kitchen and grab a bag of blood out of the fridge. When Leonidas walks in I am scrolling social media while I sip the bag. I gesture at the fridge with my phone hand, pulling the bag away from my mouth with the other, "Help yourself if you're hungry."

He grabs a bag and comes to lean against the counter next to me, I scooch a little to rest against him. His bulk is oddly comforting which makes zero sense as I was feeling crowded not ten minutes ago. I obviously need therapy. I wonder if there is a vampire therapist somewhere?

We finish our bags and he takes my bag off to the garbage with his. I watch in amazement and maybe a little suspicion, a man doing something for me instead of expecting me to do it or trying to get out of doing it. I think the suspicion is more than a little unfair, he hasn't earned the suspicion. It is certainly leftover from Fabio. Fabio was shitty enough to cover shittiness for any three or four regular men.

Instead of coming back over to stand next to me Leonidas stands at the end of the island and plants his hands on it staring down like the answers to life's questions somewhere within the countertop. Looking up at me he says, "I've been thinking."

"Well that's fucking ominous."

"Hmm, I guess it does sound that way but it really isn't. I have been thinking I want to keep you in my life. I wanted to ask how you feel about us being exclusive? Pursuing more of a relationship, if you wanted that? I find myself caring more and more about you. Wanting to spend more time with you and hoping you want to spend more time with me. How do you feel about that?"

I feel panicked and excited and I don't know if I can share how I feel about it honestly with him. "I uh, well, I wasn't expecting that." I look at the window for a moment, not that I can see out of it. "I was with my husband, Fabio, for what felt like a very long time. It was quickly very bad and stayed bad. I haven't been out of it for all that long and I am relishing the freedom. I am learning how to just be me without concern for anyone else. I do care for you. And I don't see that stopping. I feel like I need more time to be me still. And maybe explore some more. That isn't a knock on you." A deep breath and I decide to go for it, if he leaves he leaves. "If I am really honest, I feel like I am still in a head space that is really messed up. Like there is a lot of trauma I still need to process, I don't want to start a relationship that way."

He nods and exhales a shaky breath, "I understand that. Do you still want to continue on the way we have? I can wait, the beauty of being a vampire is that we have time. If you need a hundred years or so to sort yourself, well, I still want to be a part of your life. Even a shared part of your life. You are important to me, even if that means our relationship changes and you don't want anything more than friendship."

"You really mean that? Like, really *mean* that?"

He looks me in the eye, "I really mean that. Really. You are important to me and I respect that you are a person with a whole history that I know very little about. There is plenty of my history that I have yet to share, I don't expect it to be any different for you. So yeah, if friendship with no sex is what you decide you want, that is what we will have. I might need to step back for a minute to deal with my feelings about that but I would still be there if you needed me, no strings or pressure for anything more."

"Wow, I don't know what to say. No, I do know what to say. You are one of the better people I have ever known and whatever may come in the future, I definitely want you to be part of my life. However that ends up looking."

"Good. I'm glad we had this talk. Now, I need to get to work, much as I am loathe to leave."

"Oh, hey, could you drop me off on your way?"

"Of course, where do you want me to take you?"

"Dealership. I'm going to buy a car."

"Definitely. Come on hotness, let's get you to the dealership. Maybe you could swing by the jobsite later? I'll show you around, take you off into the woods." He stretches an arm out toward me and I walk over to snuggle into him, even if we aren't going to date right now, I fucking love snuggling into him.

I laugh, "Aren't you worried the big bad wolf will get me out in the woods?"

"Not even a little bit. You are way more dangerous than any wolf I know and any wolves likely to be out there work for me."

Fourteen

Leonidas

It's been a few days since I saw Jasmine last and I miss her. I think the crew would like me to go see her as well. I am noticing them giving me looks when they think I am not paying attention. Maybe I should cut out early tonight and see if she wants to see a movie or something? I'll just go ahead and finish this and let everyone know I am heading out. If Jasmine isn't interested in hanging out I'll go hunting and go home. I wonder is she would want to go hunting with me? That could be fun. She is damn sexy when she downs her prey.

"Ahem, excuse me, Leonidas?"

Oh fucking hell. I thought we were rid of Daphne. I turn to face her, "What do you want Daphne?"

She steps closer and says, "Well, I want to come back. I miss my family." She tips her head forward and looks up at me. I think it is meant to be sexy but I just find it and her repulsive. "I miss you, Leo."

Bile rises in the back of my throat but I swallow it back. "Don't call me Leo. That is not something you get to call me. Who told you I was over here anyway?" Because I am going to murder them.

"It was Haw, but I asked him. He never looked up, he may have thought he was answering someone else."

"Haw isn't here tonight. Why are you here sneaking around looking for me?"

"I told you, I miss you. I miss the gang. I guess if we are going to change things I will go along with it because I need my gang."

"Fine. You can come back on a trial basis. You fuck up even a little bit and you are done."

She squeals and jumps at me, I throw my hands up to ward her off but she grabs my neck and does her best to press her entire body against mine. Even as I am pushing her away she is trying to kiss me, all the while talking about how great I am. I hear a yelp and I finally throw this bitch off me and look up to see Jasmine. "Jasmine, wait, it isn't what you think."

Daphne grins from her spot on the ground, "It could be. Did you think I had my tongue down his throat? Cuz I definitely did."

Pointing at Daphne I tell her, "Shut your lying mouth—"

Jasmine says, "No, it's fine. You do," she gestures at us, "whatever you are doing here and I will just go. You don't owe me anything Leonidas and I don't want to be in the way of whatever you are going after now. I obviously came at a bad time."

She turns and heads for her car. I try to follow her but every fucking root in this yard trips me. I get two steps and then flat on my face again. Daphne is screaming like a banshee but I don't care, I just need to reach Jasmine before she leaves.

I hit the ground again as I hear her car start and she is backing out of the drive almost immediately. Daphne stops screaming as she speeds away, I can only hope she used her magic to take away her vocal cords. I walk out to the street and watch her taillights fade into the distance, the local flora letting me pass now. Daphne runs out into the street and throws her arms around me, I violently shove her away from me.

* * *

Jasmine

I see Daphne run out into the street and throw her arms around him as I drive away. Tears that have no business being here fill my eyes and I swipe at them. They just keep running down my face but at least I can see to drive, even if I look frightening as hell with blood tears running down my face. No one will see me right now anyway. I steer my car toward home. I don't want to be out anywhere tonight. I want to see how much alcohol it takes to get a vampire drunk. Because Leonidas really doesn't owe me anything. I told him I didn't want more when he offered it, if he found someone that offered him that, I can't even be mad at him. I can't cry at him either so maybe Scarlett and Chloe will be home to drink with me.

* * *

Jasmine

. . .

Pulling into the drive I stop and put the car in park before I turn it off. I pull down the little mirror and clean the blood off my face. Thankfully my shirt is black so the stains won't show.

Walking into the house I head for the living area and the liquor cabinet in there. Scarlett is watching a show but she presses a button on the remote and turns it off when she sees me. "What's wrong Jasmine?"

I grab a bottle of rum out of the cabinet and pour myself a glass. Setting it down so carefully I focus on the dark liquid in my cup, "Leonidas was with another girl when I got there." I feel the tears burning their way down my face again and I put the cup to my lips, tipping my head back I quickly drink it down. I am pouring another when I hear Scarlett telling someone on the phone, "Get a full order of blood and a lot of... looks like we are drinking rum tonight. Get a lot of rum." She pauses to listen while I down a second glass and then replies, "Our girl needs us tonight. Hurry up before she kills this bottle, she isn't wasting any time. I'll explain when you get here."

Scarlett sets her phone down and walks over, "Go sit down. I'll fix you a drink, you have enough of a headstart. Start talking, tell me the whole story."

I do what she says, sitting myself on the couch and grabbing a pillow to hold. I tell her everything, from me telling him I wasn't ready to finding him with another woman tonight. Scarlett hands me a rum on ice while I tell her and at some point I stop crying as the alcohol begins to numb the pain.

Scarlett asks me, "Did he tell you he wouldn't see other people?"

"No. And that is why I can't even be mad at him. He didn't say he wouldn't see other people, just that he would be there when I was ready. I thought I was fine with that. But then I saw her in his arms on the side of the job site and it just, it hurt so much. I mean, he didn't even warn me."

Chloe walks in with a brown paper bag that clinks as she walks saying, "I put the blood in the fridge but I brought the booze in here. Are we ready for refills?"

I hold my glass up after I down the rest of it, "Yes please."

She takes my glass and sets to work on that and putting away the liquor while Scarlett says, "That just doesn't sound like Leonidas. He is stuck on you, like Mikael but without the toxicity and the attempted murder. Is it possible you only saw part of a situation?"

"It is. But the real problem isn't whether or not he is with someone else, it's my reaction. I don't want to care so much. What if it turns out he is a psycho like the rest of them? I don't know if I can handle my heart being ripped out like that again. Especially so soon after the business with Mikael. I mean, at least part of me still really loved him. When he tried to kill me it hurt. That's why I was so mad, because my heart broke all over again. What if I let myself love him and he is just the same when I won't settle down with just him?"

Chloe hands me my drink and says, "We have a drunken decade or so. Preferably in a semi-remote location. Drunken vampires running about fucking with people in a city makes for headlines."

Scarlett giggles, "She's right. We'll wander off for a minute and when we come back you won't be worried about it. You'll be Leonidas who?"

"If I survive it."

"Well," Scarlett starts giggling again, "how would you not? I mean, deleting a vampire that is immune to the effects of the sun is really difficult. Not like you can dramatically walk into the sunlight and burst into flames now."

Chloe is laughing too as she says, "How anti-climactic

would that be? Dramatic exit as you talk about not wanting to live with this pain anymore and all that happens is you come back inside sweaty."

I can't help but laugh with them at the picture they painted. Scarlett nods, "We did. We've seen a few things. Done a few more. Had our own drunken decades. The point is, you will heal. Even when your world explodes into shrapnel that rips your heart into tiny bits, eventually you heal. Time is this magnificent gift that we have been given as vampires. So we use it to heal our heartbreaks and find ways to go on. Some of us even pass the knowledge on to mortals. They have to do things a little faster but it works for them too."

Chloe stares off into the distance, "Yes. Just that. We move on and we heal, from just about any damage done to us. Besides, I feel like there is something you missed. Before you, Leonidas wasn't seeing anyone. He was the leader of his gang, and he took very good care of them. But they were vicious and as you well know, they would occasionally go out and murder a trailer park. Through all that he never had anyone hanging on his arm, if he was having sex with anyone he kept it so quiet that none of the women that wanted him could find her or manage to be her even for a night. I can't swear he was celibate, but he sure as fuck seemed like it. And maybe it was just that he was really choosy about who and wasn't finding anyone. I don't know for sure. Like I said, all I do know, is that none of the vamps that wanted him have been able to catch him."

"Maybe I read it entirely wrong." I shrug, "It wouldn't be my first time being wrong. The problem is, I obviously have an issue with him being with someone else and that isn't fair to him."

Scarlett tips her head to one side, "Was it that he was with someone else or that you were surprised with it? Because those are two different things."

I look over at her, my brows drawn low as I examine my own feelings, "I- I'm not sure? I mean, I thought it was just because he was with someone else but, I mean, I don't mind the thought of it. Maybe it was the slap of the surprise. Either way, I got to get my shit together. I don't feel right about agreeing to a relationship right now, something in my gut is telling me that the usual relationship isn't going to work for me. That it isn't what I want or what I will need in the future. I don't know. I need to think about this for a while. Let's get drunk and watch cheesy romance movies. The kind that are always mostly happy and nobody ever gets left alone."

Chloe grabs the bottle and comes to sit on the couch with us, taking the other end as Scarlett is in the middle and setting the bottle on the table in front of us she grabs the remote. We pass a few hours drinking and watching these movies before Chloe stands and says she has to go, Eason is waiting for her so they can finish what they started earlier.

"Oh no! I pulled you away from sexy times? I am so sorry!"

Chloe leans down and hugs me, "Don't you worry about it. His place isn't far and I am just going to stroll over. If I message him he will meet me on the way, maybe we'll do naughty things in a wooded area for kicks." She grins, hugs Scarlett and heads for the door.

I grab the bottle off the table and refill our glasses, "A toast to Chloe and Eason, may their sex be fantastic for both of them and may they not be caught fucking in public!"

We clink glasses carefully and drink, but my aim is garbage so far into the third bottle and I feel some of my rum dribble down my chin and onto my breast. Scarlett's voice is husky when she says, "Need some help getting that spill?"

Her eyes are dark like the moon and her voice sends a

shiver down my spine to pool in warm places. I pull my neckline down a little more with both hands, "Yes, please."

My consent was all she needed and her head dipped down, her lips just touching the rise of one breast before her tongue darts out to lap at the rum. My core clenches and my nipples harden with expectation, I lean into her just fractionally. Her hands cover mine as she continues to lick the rum down into the valley between my breasts she guides my hands in slipping my shirt down to give her better access.

When my shirt won't go any farther she whispers, her breath tickling my skin, "Are you very attached to this shirt?"

In answer I rip my shirt open down the front, leaving her path unimpeded except for the bra I wear. I feel her hands skimming my rib cage as she reaches behind me, unclasping my bra. Her hands are quickly shoving my bra up and out of her way as her mouth lays claim to a nipple while a hand cups the other breast, thumb and finger rolling the nipple gently between them.

My hands release my shirt and start to roam her body, she sits back, grabbing my hands with her own she pins them to my sides and goes back to my breasts, nipping one she says, "Not yet. I have wanted to explore you for entirely too long." Kissing her way up my chest and to my neck she nips me there and I moan, my head falling away to give her better access. "Not yet. I know how you love to be bitten there, I want to know where else you like to be bitten." She kisses along my jawline, I turn my head to meet her lips with mine. She kisses me long and hard, her body presses against mine curves and softness meeting and smashing against each other.

She breaks the kiss, "Let's go upstairs."

"Are you going to tie me up?"

"I can. I might spank you too, if you want those things."

"I do."

"Let's go."

Getting upstairs takes some time, her hands roam my body in the most delicious ways and I keep stopping to let her. We finally make it to my room and she tells me, "Get naked and get in that bed. I will be right back."

I do as she ordered, stripping off my clothing and getting on the bed. The wait isn't long as she enters the room with rope and some other things I don't pay much attention to as she sets them on the foot of the bed she keeps the rope in one hand and I hold my wrists out to her. She wraps and ties them, her movements swift and sure. She pushes them toward the headboard when she finishes, then she is over me saying, "If at any time it is too much, say so. If I make you uncomfortable, say so. I'll stop. If you want it harder, say that too."

I nod and bring my face toward hers, "I promise, I will make noise. Now touch me dammit."

She kisses me hard, pushing my head back into the pillow as she does. Her hand reaches down to pinch a nipple and it responds immediately but her hand keeps moving. Skimming down my rib cage and belly she rest her hand on my mound. My legs spread of there own accord, my hips pressing up. She breaks the kiss, moving her legs between mine as she kisses her way down to lave my breasts. My head is spinning with pleasure, my moans fill the room. She abandons my breasts to nibble her way down my torso, each bite is electrifying. My body feels like an instrument finally being played by a master musician. She pushes my legs as far apart as they will go, I bend them at the knees to give myself traction as I lift my hips and push my aching pussy toward her. She leans down and blows on it ever so gently and I groan in frustration.

Her hands cup my ass squeezing softly. I can feel her mouth hovering over me and I open my eyes to see why, as soon as she meets my eyes she flicks her tongue out, hitting my clit and making my whole body shiver with the pleasure. A thumb plays at the dripping wet entrance to my pussy, teasing, teasing. My hips don't know if they should press up to her mouth or down to ride that thumb. She solves the problem by pressing her thumb in as she sucks my clit hard into her mouth and my orgasm throws me off a cliff to soar into a million glowing pieces.

Fifteen

Jasmine

Waking up the next evening with Scarlett still in my bed I can't say I am at all annoyed. I feel like I need to go apologize to Leonidas for running out like that and maybe for having the plants trip him up. I will, I will apologize to him and tell him it isn't my business but I would like some warning. And that I won't show up unannounced like that. This whole thing was really on me.

For now though, I think I am going to enjoy cuddling with Scarlett as we both finish waking up. I snuggle further into her arms as they tighten slightly around me, she whispers, "Good evening."

"Good evening to you."

"I guess we need to talk now. Figure out where we go from here."

"Yeah…" I sigh.

Scarlett clears her throat and says, "I don't really want to be with any one person, and I think we are in agreement on that?"

"We are. And I think our friendship is way more important than the fantastic fucking."

"Girl, same. So, we are just going to be aware that we are both exploring other people and that we may have relationships with them too. That way we have no misunderstandings."

"Perfect. I need to go find Leonidas and apologize. I feel really bad about the running away and all the tripping him."

"What? Tripping him?"

"Well, I didn't want him to follow me so I used my magic and tripped him with roots. Repeatedly."

Scarlett chuckles, "That is great. So chasing you is out. Anything else I should know?"

"I think you found most of it last night."

She tweaks my nipple, "Maybe we should see what else we can find about each other sometime soon."

"I wouldn't mind another exploratory session before I head out to find Leonidas. I think I may have missed some spots during round two."

Her hand glides down my body to stroke my pussy, "Sounds like a great way to start the evening."

Sixteen

Leonidas

Damn Daphne. Her fucking antics last night got Jasmine's tail in a twist and she managed to fuck up two windows before she got out to the street where I was watching Jasmine drive away.

I had no choice but to stay and fix that, though I did have the guys get Daphne the fuck away from me and I had her put to work mixing mud for the walls around the back yard. She wasn't happy but that suited my mood. Especially when she went home near morning covered in mud.

I had to retreat home then too, keeping my immunity to the sun a secret is a must. The day was long as I waited, only falling asleep around mid-afternoon. The sun is down now though and I am on my way to Jasmine's. She is going to talk to me dammit.

I see her car in the drive as I pull up and I think briefly about pulling in behind it to block her in, but decide against being shit. I get to the front door and knock, waiting for what seems forever. When the door opens it is Chloe on the other side.

"Hi Chloe, I need to talk to Jasmine, can I see her please?"

"Um, no. You hurt her feelings last night with your girl-friend surprise."

"That thing was not, is not, my girlfriend."

"Well, she still isn't available right now. I can tell her you stopped by."

"Chloe, come on, it isn't what she thinks it was. I swear. Please go get her, let me explain to her."

"Not a chance."

"Ugh. Ok." I drag a hand through my hair, "Can I leave her a note or something?"

She crosses her arms, "I suppose. But I want to know what happened. Your side."

"Sure! Let me get my..." I pat my pockets for my work notepad and pencil, finding it in a back pocket I scrawl a quick note asking her to please call me, meet with me, something so I can explain. Handing it over to Chloe I start telling her what happened. I emphasize that Daphne is not someone that I would ever have anything to do with in that way. By the time I leave, she still looks skeptical but she didn't throw my note back at me or try to kill me so I figure it will probably get to Jasmine.

Seventeen

Jasmine

Wandering downstairs I head for the kitchen first thing. I am starving. Blood bag in hand I meet Chloe on my way to the livingroom.

"I have a note for you from Leonidas. He came by this morning looking for you. I put him off."

"Oh no, I have got to call him and apologize. I really over-reacted, it should not have been that big a deal, it was just a surprise is all."

Before Chloe can respond someone pounds on the door like the police. I shove note and phone in my back pocket as Chloe and I head for the door, Scarlett meets us there. I open the door to find two massive vampires standing in the door-way, Chloe asks, "Who are you?"

Massive number one pulls a card out of his pocket and passes it over to her. The front reads 'Enforcer' while the back reads, 'Please see the council for further information'.

Scarlett says, "Great. Ok Enforcer, are you capable of speech or do you have a card to explain why you are here?"

He grunts like he found that funny but doesn't remember how to laugh, in a surprisingly high voice he tells us, "I am here to inform Jasmine," his eyes come to rest on me, "of her invitation to come before the council and answer to the charges against her."

Before I can stop myself I blurt out, "What fucking charges? Surely this council doesn't concern itself with the ones I remove from making the mortals miserable!"

Another grunt, "Your charges are being a magic user and using that magic to force a vampire to turn you. Plotting to take over the council. Attempted murder of one of our own kind to hide your secrets. And being able to walk in the sunlight. I am obligated to inform you that if you do not show up for your appointed hearing date we will be forced to come find you and bring you to face your crimes."

"Well fuck you, I'll be there with bells on, I did nothing wrong. And that was self defense! He tried to murder me first, he's just bad at it."

Another grunt, this time his shoulders twitch. The two turn to leave without so much as a goodbye an I yell after them, "Wait, where do I go? You didn't give me an address!"

The silent one walks back and hands me a card with an address on it. "Thanks, I guess." I take the card and close the door behind me as he turns and walks away into the night.

I stare at the card in my hands like it might give me the answers to what the hell is going on but it remains silent in my hands, any secrets it has it isn't sharing. They know about everything. Their is only one way they could know about it all, including my being immune to the sunlight. Mikael. The only other people that know, have as much or more to lose that me if things come out.

But Mikael would definitely believe that he could get away with ratting me out and suffer no consequences himself. I might really kill him this time if I make it through this. Holy fuck. How—

"Helloooo? Jasmine? Are you in there? You're smoking. It would be great if you didn't set the house on fire." I come back from my dark thoughts and see Scarlett waving her hand in front of my face, the room is smoky.

"Shit, I'm sorry." I tell her as I rope in my magic and work at clearing the room of smoke. "I was just thinking about how this could have happened."

Chloe says, "Oh we know how it happened. Who else would do something so shitty as to report you to the council? Four people know besides Mikael. Of those four, three have gotten the immunity to sunlight from you, and thank you so much for that it is amazing. The other one is your mentor. She believes you to be the person of the prophecy that is going to save the world. Not much chance of her turning you in, especially not to the vampire council."

"That is where I went with it and I was imagining creative ways to kill Mikael."

Scarlett gives me a gentle push toward the living room and does the same to Chloe as she says, "Come on, lets go sit down and figure it out, there is no reason to stand in the hall for this."

In the living room I sit in a chair, my magical control is not good enough for anyone to sit next to me while I feel so volatile. I see a flash of something on Scarlett's face and Chloe giving me a look, I probably just hurt her feelings. Shit. "I'm going to sit over here because I still feel pretty violent and I don't want to risk hurting either of you because my control over my magic isn't great. You both are more important to me than getting comfort from sitting closer to you."

Scarlett's face lifts and Chloe gives me a quick thumbs up

before saying, "So we know that this was Mikael. But you probably know nothing about the council, right?"

"Right. Today is the first I remember hearing of them. Why is there a vampire council anyway?"

Scarlett answers my question, "Because over time the majority of new vampires began to be white men. Many of whom are greedy, petulant, spoiled, and wildly egotistical. The vampire world was kind of overrun with them for a while. That's how people got so frightened of vampires, because bodies were piling up and these guys all thought they were kings of their own little countries and nothing bad could possibly happen to them. When the vampire hunters began to pop up, they didn't concern themselves with them beyond killing the ones that showed up. However, all of the older vampires had been watching this with a great deal of trepidation, though they were unwilling to act until the hunters started popping up. That was when the call went out. All the elders met in a remote, forgotten castle. That was when it was decided that there must be a faction of vampires that would decide the fate of those that called attention to our kind, along with some other rules. So the council was born and they are the final decision in all things because so many of us remember what it was like to hide in caves and to bury ourselves in the woods for fear of being staked while we slept. The council went out and found those that had caused the terror in the mortal world, they killed them and left the bodies near hunters, splashing the blood on them as well to make it appear that they did the killing. The hunters knew of course that they didn't do it but they accepted the credit. One of them, Van Helsing was the worst. He sort of followed the council, though he was only trying to track down vampires.

His luck held and he became known as a fantastic hunter of the vampire. He wrote all these silly stories full of lore about us, most of which were completely false. His career ended abruptly, but he was old by then so it was no hardship for him. He thought he had magically rid the world of vampires. Since then, the members of the council have changed every one hundred years. While a vampire can serve more than one term, they may not serve them consecutively with the exception of dire circumstances. No one under 500 years old may serve and some are not permitted to serve no matter their age due to a general inability to handle power of any kind."

"Oh wow. That really happened? I mean, I'm not surprised but just...damn. I don't understand being that oblivious."

Chloe nods, "Well, they managed it. And it was that fuckery Van Helsing wrote that got the church involved. Once they believed they had eradicated vampires they turned to the next logical enemy of the church, women. They went after every woman with a modicum of independence, called her a witch and got rid of her in the most horrifying ways they could dream up. Very few of the women they burnt or tortured to death were actual witches. They saw it coming long before it happened and they left. Witches don't need civilization, they just enjoy it like we do. They took as many women away with them as they could convince to go. But they knew they would never get them all away, so they focused on helping the ones that would be helped."

"Fuck. That must have been hard. Leaving, knowing that so many would die."

"The ones I met," Scarlett goes to the liquor cabinet and raises a glass at us, we both nod yes, "they were scarred from it. Some of them ended up with a life long hatred of the church for the power they wielded so carelessly and with so little thought for life. Some of the ones they burned came back as young witches with a lot of fire. The consequences of those vampire's actions have been far reaching indeed. That is why the council was formed and why it has stayed in place to this day. It is for the safety of the entire world."

"Okay. But what do I do about them? I don't really want to die for the sins of some guys that couldn't figure out how to act right and I especially don't want to die for the sin of not being Mikael's toy."

"Well," Scarlett hands our drinks to us as she goes back to her seat, "you aren't the first magic user to ever become a vampire. The council doesn't appreciate it overmuch, but you can tell them that you didn't know you had magic prior to being turned. They can verify with your teacher how she found you and decided to start training you. They will be glad to know you are being responsible and learning how to control your magic. That will be points in your favor. I suggest you let them see your natural reaction to the idea of taking over the world," she points at me, "exactly that face you are making right now. Tell them how you feel about running things. Nobody that knows what managing things is like is going to believe you want anything to do with running the whole damn world. The only thing I see that could be an issue is the sunlight. There is only one way to test that. Can you make it look like you are burning as the sunlight touches you? Give yourself a temporary allergy to the sun? Make an illusion? Something?"

"Um, maybe?" I take a swig of my drink, "It might be beyond my skill level. I'll message Helen, see if she knows a way for me to do it. Man, I hope I don't have to actually set myself on fire." Pulling ot my phone I message Helen, giving her a run down on the problem at hand and what I want to do should the need arise. "Is it possible that they will just skip over that, after finding out for certain how much he already lied about everything else?"

Chloe chews her lip a little, "It is possible. When I... Ah hell, not like you won't eventually know. When I was on the council, we wouldn't have gone through that. But some of the current council are a little more easily swayed, they may want to find something he didn't lie about to save face after they pushed for the hearing."

"I guess I just need to wait for Helen to message me back. She's probably working at the bookstore right now."

Eighteen

Mikael

My phone rings, Daphne's name on the screen. She better have something good to report if I have to listen to her voice. "Hello Daphne."

"Mikael, hi! Things have gone so much better than I could have planned."

"Oh really? Will this be a short and lucrative assignment for you?"

"I think it might be."

"Do go on, tell me what has happened."

"I went to the jobsite Leonidas is working on. Convinced him to let me back in, that was easy as pie. Then, I smelled a woman's perfume on the breeze and I threw myself on him. I was in luck, the woman was Jasmine! She came around the corner to see us appearing to be all over each other. She got out of there like her tale was on fire. Leonidas tried to go after her but kept tripping over stuff. That was weird, but whatever. I broke the two windows he had just installed, so he had to stay there for the rest of the night. I followed him home, then hid nearby so I could be there when he woke up. I followed him when he left his house and he went straight to Jasmine's place. Where he was turned away!"

"Oh, you did do well. I assume you have her address for me? What did she say when she saw you two together?"

"She said something about making a mistake and that she would leave us alone. Her address is 4598 Raptor Lane."

I jot that down on my desk blotter, "Excellent. Could you hear any of the conversation about why he was turned away? Was it Jasmine that answered the door?" I find the desire for her, the desire to have her is just as strong now. Seeing the address on paper, I know I am going to have no choice but to go to her. I realize Daphne is still talking and I cut her off saying, "I'm so sorry, I wasn't listening. Would you please repeat that?"

"Thinking about your lady, huh? Yeah, I can say it again. It wasn't Jasmine that answered the door. Looked like one of your old boarders, Chloe. I couldn't really hear what they were saying, I was worried that if I put my window down they would notice. He left a note but she just put it in her pocket. I don't think Jasmine is going to get it."

"Wonderful. That suits my plans perfectly." The itch to see Jasmine is growing. I need to claim her for my own. To teach her that I am the one she belongs with, now and forever. "I must go now Daphne, your payments will be transferred shortly. Do keep an eye on the situation, report back if you find anything else of import."

She is happily nattering away as I tell her bye and hang up. I don't worry that she'll be offended because once Vigo sends her the money, she'll forget that I hung up on her.

* * *

Jasmine

Our conversation has fallen silent as we all contemplate the ramifications of the council hearing. A knock sounds at the door and I look at them, "You expecting anyone?"

They both shake their heads no as Eason walks in, "Hey, you want me to get that?"

Scarlett and I both look at Chloe, she grins. I shrug, "You know, considering the last visitor, maybe we should all be there to answer it. Be like that movie Clue." I chuckle at my joke as I get up. Everyone else just looks confused at the reference. Guess we need a movie night.

Opening the door with everyone behind me, Mikael was the last thing I expected to see, yet there he stood. "Jasmine! So good to see you, I've missed you so much!" I am frozen with shock as Mikael leans into our house and hugs me, pulling me close to him. He smells nice and his body feels good against mine, but the pain blooms in my chest, like he was stabbing me all over again. I can't, I can't have him touching me. My shock paralysis broken I bring my hands up and shove, breaking his hold on me. I see the shock and anger cross his face, though he schools his features quickly.

"What are you doing here Mikael? Come to try to kill me again? Or see if the council has been by?"

His mouth turns down at the corners, "That hurts Jasmine. I would never do such a thing. I haven't had any dealings with the council in a very long time. I came to see you. I miss you, I miss us."

"Mikael, you tried to murder me right after having sex with me. That means you don't get to miss me. Or, well, you can miss me all you want but I don't give a fuck. You don't get me. You don't get to show up at my house that you weren't ever invited to and tell me that you miss me. Fuck off and go somewhere else."

"Jasmine, I am trying to be patient with you. But this nonsense with you living elsewhere, it has got to stop. You need to come home where you belong." He sticks his hand out like I am some obstinate child refusing to get in the car. "Come, we'll go home and you can tell me all about your adventures."

I am dumbfounded by his obliviousness. "No. Not ever. I will not be with you ever again Mikael. And I sure as fuck am not going anywhere with you. How did you even find out where I live?"

"I tire of your attitude." Mikael grabs my arm and tries to snatch me forward saying, "Come on!"

My left hand swings before I can think about it, planting itself in his face with a satisfying crunch as an arm snakes around my waist, stopping him from pulling me forward. His hand is ripped off my arm at the same moment. The shock on his face as his nose is repairing itself is priceless.

"I told you Mikael, you don't own me. I will not be going with you now or ever. Fuck off. Don't come back here. You are not welcome."

"Jasmine, this is your last chance. You come willingly now or it will go badly for you." His face is cold and calculating, "This seems like a nice house. Be shame if something were to happen to it."

"Get. The. Fuck. Off. My. Property." I say and the magic roiling in my blood slips its leash, sending him tumbling in a gust of wind that pushes him right off the property.

When the gust disappears he rights himself, and turns to face me, "You'll beg to come back soon and I will make you grovel before I allow you back. Your behavior today has guaranteed that."

"Fuck off Mikael." I say as the arm around my waist snatches me back out of the doorway and Scarlett shuts the door in front of me.

The arm around my waist releases me and I turn to see Eason behind me, but he is watching Chloe tap on her phone. I watch too as she stops and Mikael's voice plays from it. Chloe starts dancing, "I got the whole thing! We have a recording of him not only denying that he contacted the council, but swearing violence on you, trying to kidnap you, and not denying that he tried to kill you! The council is going to crucify him!"

* * *

We are still celebrating the video when there is another knock on the door. Eason opens the door, and says, "Hey Leonidas!"

Chloe says, "Oh shit! Leonidas! I forgot to give you his note! Here," she digs into a pocket, "I'm so sorry." She hands over a note, folded and slightly crumpled. I turn to the door, Leonidas looks upset.

"I'm so sorry Leonidas, come in." I walk over and give him a quick hug, so he knows that I am not in any way upset with him. I shouldn't have left it this long without calling him. "Come on, let's go upstairs," I stop and turn, "I think we were pretty well done talking about everything anyway, right?"

Scarlett and Chloe both nod. Scarlett says, "Completely. We'll see you in the morning." She blows me a kiss and I blow one back at her before I take Leonidas' arm again and we start up the stairs.

"Listen, I want to apologize. I was surprised and I really had no right to act like that. I insisted we remain free agents. I can't be upset because you have someone else too and—"

"Wait. You have it all wrong. I agree with what you said,

except the part about me being with that woman," he shudders, "that is never happening. I have a bunch of reasons why but they don't matter. She is not someone I would ever be intimate with."

I shut my bedroom door behind us and move to sit in the middle of my bed, "Well, now I am confused. You looked really intimate when I walked up."

He shoves a hand through his hair, "I know. I had been working over there when she showed up, wanting to be back in the clan. I allowed it and was just about to send her off to talk to one of my guys about putting her to work when the scent of you reached us. Just as I lifted my nose to the wind to breathe deeper, she pounced on me."

"Oh holy shit. I'm a terrible person. I didn't realize you were being attacked right then. I would have helped you. I am so sorry. I shouldn't have judged a situation I didn't know anything about. Can you forgive me?"

"Gods yes! I came here hoping you would forgive me. Let's just call it a misunderstanding and move on."

"I agree. And I will wait to at least find out what is going on, instead of assuming things and running off."

"Perfect, now what was the very serious conversation that you needed to check in with your friends to be sure you all were done talking about it?"

"Ugh. That is a whole story, but real quick before I tell you all those news, I am having a friends with benefits situation with Scarlett."

"Nice, thanks for letting me know. So what's the news?"

I tell him about the council summons delivered tonight, about Mikael's visit, and all that happened with that. His eyes are wide while I tell him about the summons but narrowed and possibly glowing a little as I relate the story of Mikael trying to kidnap me.

"You know he won't stop. For so long as Mikael is alive you are not safe. He will keep doing things like this. Snitching to the council, trying to own you. I have to tell you, if I see him out and about, I am going to end him. Hopefully you will eventually forgive me, but I just can't let him keep wandering about fucking with you."

"Leonidas, you say the sweetest things. You're right, I would forgive you really quickly. It would solve a lot of problems of which he is directly responsible. While I don't want to kill him myself, I would feel the same way if someone from your past was harassing you in a manner similar to this. Now, it looks to me like we had an argument. Feels like there is something people do to make up after a fight, got any ideas about what that should be?"

Leonidas steps over to the bed and kicks his boots off before hopping on the bed. In a flash he is leaning over me and I am pressed back on the pillows as he says, "I can think of a few things, but I believe we have entirely too much clothing on to do it justice. May I help you out of your clothing ma'am?"

Snatching my shirt up and off I toss it toward the other side of the room, "Race you?"

He growls and snatches my leggings down my body as I unclasp my bra, he watches me toss it away as he does the same with my leggings, "You win. Now you get a prize."

He lifts me off the bed to bury his face between my breasts. I lose the ability to care who wins or loses as he moves to take a nipple in his mouth and suck hard before biting the other nipple, my flesh pebbling all over my body from the sensations.

My hands roam the muscular expanse of his shoulders and down his back as he nibbles his way up my chest and to the sensitive bundle of nerves that lives at the junction of neck and shoulder. He bites me as he lays me back on the bed, my body arching with the pleasure of it. He withdraws his fangs, the bite having brought me nearly to the edge and he whispers, "Not yet. Not yet." I groan in frustration then his hand slides up my thigh, his thumb coming to rest on my pussy. Rocking my hips to press into his hand but he only chuckles as he maintains the lightest of touches.

His chuckle lights another fire in me and bringing my hands to his chest I push up and roll us so I am on top. Sitting up I say, "So you want to tease? Well, you first." His eyes get dark as I lean forward, pressing my breasts to his chest and my lips to his. Little kisses along his jawline, my hands on his shoulders as I rock my hips, sliding back and forth along the length of his cock. His breathing gets faster as I curve my back to line us up only to slide back without giving him entrance. Raising myself I begin to kiss my way down his body, alternating kisses with bites. He is panting by the time I get my mouth to his cock. I lick the length of it, tasting myself on him. His hips thrust upward as I move back from him, "Not yet sir, not yet."

He groans, and I take his cock in my hands, bringing it to my lips I engulf the head, watching as his hands grip the sheets. Taking a breath I deep throat him as far as I can quickly, sucking hard as I lift my mouth away from his pelvis. His moans and the way his body is shaking as I repeat the pattern have me so hot I think I could come from a touch. Lifting myself I crawl over him to position myself, he has reached down and taken his own cock in his hand to line it up with my entrance. I feel it bouncing ever so slightly upward as I hover over him. Lowering myself slowly onto him, I feel the glorious stretch. The filling as I move down slow to prolong the sensation.

My eyes are closed and my nails digging lightly into his

chest when I reach the base. I sit there a moment longer just to enjoy the feeling. Raising my hips I start to ride him, the pace slow at first but picking up speed with every stroke. He presses his thumb to my clit, his fingers resting on my belly as he moves it in small circles, sending electricity coursing through my body. Every time our bodies meet his thumb presses hard on my clit, my pussy clenches around his cock.

The orgasm takes me by surprise, I am frozen in ecstasy as he moves his hands to grip my hips and fuck me hard till he reaches his peak, increasing my pleasure. As the stars recede I melt down to lay on his chest unmoving. He wraps his arms around me and we lay there, unmoving as our breathing returns to normal.

Laying there, my mind drifting, I realize I feel really safe here with him and that scares the hell out of me. He starts to move and says, "Loathe as I am to do this, I need to get to work."

I seize on that and lift myself off of him, trying to keep the relief from showing on my face. I don't want to hurt his feelings with my issues. Moving off to the side I crawl off the bed and visit the bathroom. I take the few moments while I clean up to get my head right, at least enough to keep it together till he is gone. Exiting the bathroom I grab a robe and slip my arms into it while he visits the bathroom. He comes out dressed and damn, I want to keep him here. Then that fear tries to rise up, I shove it down and walk over while he shoves his feet into his boots. Straightening he takes in my robe and says, "Damn. You sure do make it hard on a man trying to leave." Pulling me into his arms he kisses me long and hard, by the time he releases me I am ready to take him back to bed, fear be damned. "Is it ok to come here in the morning? Or would you like to come to my place? If you are comfortable with that?"

I want to say no and at the same time everything in me is pushing for a yes, "Um, yes. You can come here. I think I would like to have you here." His smile is brilliant as he gives me a quick kiss and tells me he has to go, he is really late as it is. I watch as he leaves, listening as he bounds down the stairs and lets himself out the front door. I hear his truck start up and pull away from the house and I release the breath I have been holding.

Dropping my robe I crawl back into my bed and try to ignore the voice telling me I am in danger, even with the risk of Leonidas hurting me I don't think I can let him go.

Nineteen

Jasmine

I wake to the sound of an explosion, as I fly through the air before my bed and I hit the far wall. I smell the smoke as I fight my way out of the crush of bed, sheets, wall, and rubble. My ears are ringing a little and I can see daylight through the missing corner of my bedroom. I am still dressed enough, my pajamas are only a little worse for the wear. I look around and spot my purse strap sticking out from under some other stuff. I grab it and head for my door. I step into the hallway to find Scarlett, Chloe, and Eason just making it to my end of the house. Chloe asks, "What the hell happ—" and another explosion rocks the house.

"We need to get out of here, explanations later!"

I follow behind them, blocking the flames from reaching us as we look for a way out. The front of the house is a mass of flames, both back corners are equally trashed. We end up in the living room, I tell them, "We'll have to go out the window!"

The flames are starting to creep at the edges of the door when Eason says, "We can't leave, the sun will fry us!"

Chloe, Scarlett, and I look at each other. I say, "There's no time for another way. He has to be brought in or he is going to die."

They nod and Chloe turns to Eason, "I know this sounds crazy, but I need you to drink from Jasmine here and then just trust me. I promise, you won't burn up."

Eason looks very skeptical, but sees the flames creeping past the barrier I put up, "Ok, sure. If theres any chance I'll take it."

I step over to him and let him drink from my wrist, no time for the enjoyable bites. He drinks delicately and agonizingly slow. I am jittery as I watch the flames crawling across the ceiling. Finally, I think he has had enough and I tap his shoulder. He releases my wrist and Scarlett snatches the curtain open. Eason throws his arms up as the sun hits him but he doesn't burn up. That is enough for us. I don't know if it will work but I wrap a shield around us all and focus really hard on no one seeing us as we dash for the small wooded area behind the house.

* * *

In the woods we stop to regroup while Eason explores his new ability to tolerate the sun. I flop down to sit on a log and gather my wits. Scarlett looks at Chloe, "We can't be wandering around during the day. If the wrong people see us..."

Chloe hugs herself, "I know. We have to lay low somewhere for the day. This barely counts as a woodsy spot for children, it won't work for us at all. What about the library? We could hide in one of the darker corners till closing."

Eason looks at us, "We aren't really dressed for it, and we smell like smoke. We need someone to deliver us clothing. Maybe deliver us."

"I think I might be able to make that happen. Does anyone have a phone?"

Scarlett hands hers over, "I was playing on my phone when the first explosion happened."

I tap in Leonidas' number. It rings twice before he answers, "Knight Construction."

"Hello Leonidas, I need a big favor."

"Jasmine? Why are you calling me from someone else's phone?"

"Well, that's a long story. The short version is my house went boom and we need to be discreetly picked up from the little copse of trees on Purgatory Lane and taken somewhere safer than here."

"Ok. My house is safe and I was just leaving work. I stayed late this morning. You want me to come get you?"

"I was hoping you could send one of the wolves? Maybe one of the ones that helped me move that day? I worry that we are being watched, and I don't want any more of us to be incriminated if we are."

"Sure, I'll send Banner. He drives a dark tinted mini van. Flames down the side. I just messaged him, he says he'll be there in five. I told him to bring you all straight to my house and I will be there when you arrive. Unless you are followed, then lose the tail and get here."

"Thanks, we'll see you in a bit." I hand Scarlett her phone back, "Ok, guessing you heard both ends of that but, Banner is coming to get us. Let's move over to that side. A mini van with flames down the side..." I chuckle as I walk over to the far side of the copse. We stop while still inside the tree line. Our wait is short, within a minute or two we see this blue minivan, shiny and tinted with flames rolling down the side. I can see the window is cracked slightly, I know he is scenting us.

He rolls to a stop in front of us and the side door rolls open. I look up and down the street, seeing no one peering out their windows or wandering about I dart into the van. Everyone else follows suit behind me and the door slides shut as Banner starts the van rolling forward again.

I move up to the front seat and sit down, "Hey Banner, how's things?"

"Good, good. I hear someone blew up your house. Who'd you piss off?"

"If I had to guess, I would say Mikael. But that may just be me blaming him because he is behind so many other things. I don't have any solid evidence beyond the fact that he found us last night and today our house blew up."

"That is pretty incriminating. I'm assuming your homes don't usually blow up. Me and the boys could go round and have a sniff later. It's pretty smoky out there, but vampire scents tend to be exaggerated for us. Luckily most of you smell good." He cuts his eyes at me, "Though some of you go well beyond the realm of smelling good. Fucking hell, do you bathe in something extra?"

I can hear my companions giggling in the back, "Nothing out of the ordinary. Just some regular soap. No special scents or anything."

"Fucking hell. You smell good through the smoke. I think it may add to it in a weird way. Those assholes in the back smell like burnt house and spices that are out of date. You, you smell wild roses and earth and rain and smoke, but it all just blends into this fantastic scent instead of the smoke overpowering everything and making the usual scents less."

"Um. I don't know. Want me to put down a window?" I tell him that but I have an idea. I think it may be the magic. I think it absorbs things and changes them in ways that I don't understand at all. Maybe I never will.

"Nah, we are here." He says as we pull up in front of an old gothic house, gray with dark brown shingles. It is gorgeous. I have seen it before, just never in the daylight.

"Thanks Banner!" I tell him as I lean over and give him a hug, he groans as he wraps his arms around me and inhales deeply.

He releases me with, "Go before I decide to keep you."

I laugh and hop out of the van, shutting the door behind me. Everyone else piles out onto the sidewalk, thanking Banner and closing the door once they are all out.

As Banner drives away we walk toward the house and Leonidas opens the door. "Nice pajamas," he says, crossing his arms in front of his chest.

I lean up on my toes and kiss his cheek, "Didn't you know that smoke and soot stained Lamb Chops pajamas are all the rage right now?"

He laughs and grabs me up in his arms, "Come on everyone, let's get you all sorted and you can tell me why your house blew up." He presses a kiss to my neck, making me shiver before he sets me down and ushers us all inside.

The explanations go quickly, and Eason offers for all of us to stay at the house the guys bought.

Leonidas says, "They could stay here, very few people know where I live."

Eason nods, "No one knows where we live. And, there are four of us to keep watch. You have to go to work, while we are older and established our fortunes some time ago. Let us protect Jasmine. You are welcome to come to our home as well. Though I will ask that you watch to ensure that you are not followed."

Leonidas nods, "I don't like it, but you're right."

Twenty

Jasmine

Today is the day. I have a Lyft taking me to near the place, I'll walk the rest of it. I figure the council will be less than okay with it if I get dropped at the door. I have the video of Mikael stored in my messages and I plan to show it to them today, to fight fire with fire, so to speak. See how he likes getting his own summons to the council. I sincerely doubt they like being used to harass women so some ignorant asshole can own her.

The car stops and I thank the driver before I get out. They put down the window on the passenger side to say, "Ma'am, I don't mean to intrude but are you sure you want ot be left out here? This isn't the greatest neighborhood."

I smile, "Oh, thank you for your concern. I'll be all right. Have a good night."

They drive off with a shrug and I continue on my way. The building is easy to find, one knock and the door is opened. I find one of the guys that delivered the summons waiting on the other side of the door. "Well, fancy meeting you here. Will you be escorting me to the council?"

His lips twitch and he says, "Yes. Please come with me."

I laugh, "Sir, we have barely met! You are at leat going to need to take me out somewhere first. But I will take your arm and walk with you."

He blushes, holy shit I made the big bad vampire blush! He lifts his arm and I place mine on his as he guides me through the maze that is the council building. We arrive at a double doored room and he opens a door to admit me into the room. I enter to find the room bare of anything except a long crescent shaped desk that people I assume are the council are sitting behind. The guy that walked me in whispers, "Go stand in the middle of the room." Then he closes the door behind me.

I walk slowly to the middle of the room, studying the faces of the council. Most of them look approachable, a couple seem disgusted by me. That could be a problem. I reach the middle of the room and one of the women in the middle of the crescent speaks, "Hello Jasmine. I am Felicity, to my right are Rick, Scott, and Tiara. To my left are Barret, Bianca, and Brian. We will be listening to your defense of the accusations made against you. First, are you a practitioner of magic also known as a witch?"

"Yes I am."

"Were you a witch when you were turned?"

"Not that I know of."

"I see, could you explain?"

"Yes. I was just a regular human until I was turned. I only decided I wanted to be turned because it solved a whole lot of problems for me. Right then I was the only surviving witness to a rather large vampire feeding. I found Mikael under my trailer while I was running from the other guy. It was a day or so later, at Mikael's house when I decided I wanted to be a vampire. The other guy was planning to kill me and I did not want to spend the rest of my mortal life locked away hiding. The other guy only wanted to make sure I wasn't going to draw attention to vampires. So, becoming a vampire solved that problem."

"I see. And when did the magic come into play?"

"I didn't know about the magic until I went to an all night book store. The people running it are witches and the one working the register that night was very concerned because she said I was leaking magic all over the place. She became my teacher, my magic mentor. She can verify my story, her name is Helen Bastelle."

The lady at the left end says, "I know Helen. She did recently say that she had acquired a new student because they were leaking magic all over her book store."

Felicity says, "Thank you Barret. And have you been training since then? Learning to control your magic rather than be controlled by it?"

"I have. I don't want to hurt anyone I didn't intend to hurt."

Felicity looks at her fellow council members and says, "I think we can all agree that you are not working to take over the world being a vampiric witch. However, the matter of whether or not you can walk in the sun with immunity is still up for debate."

The second guy from the right says, "I think we should bring in a UV light a put it to the test. She'll heal quickly enough if she isn't immune and if she is then we will know that much faster. We can decide what to do with her and be done with this."

Felicity narrows her eyes at him, "Scott, you sound less than impartial. Do you know this woman?"

Scott huffs, "No! I am bloody tired of these questions and being so soft. Once upon a time we would have eliminated anyone that was a potential threat to our kind. Now we must question them and play nice, almost like we were mortals!"

The woman second from the left end says, "Scott, you are excused. Your judgement is skewed in this case, you cannot be an impartial judge."

Scott explodes from his seat, "Fuck you Bianca! Just because you are leader this time doesn't mean shit! You are still a know nothing by-blow of a minor lordling with less brains than a rooster! I should go kill this bitch now and solve the damn problem myself!" He turns toward me and I see the bunching of his muscles, I know he is about to try and carry out his threat. I slam up a barrier of air all around me and then everything disappears into a darkness so deep even my vampire eyes can't see anything.

When the light returns Hekate stands between me and the council, pale faces suddenly more serious and Scott slides back into his seat very slowly.

Hekate looks at each of the council members in turn, and while I can smell the fear in all of them, to their credit they hold themselves in check. Hekate inhales deeply with a smile, letting them all know she can smell their fear, "I have been watching this little hearing with great interest. I was not going to interfere as long as reason prevailed. Since it is not, here I am."

Scott manages to become more pale at her statement and Hekate's smile grows cruel, "Yes boy, you are tipping the balance with your shenanigans. I think you will need to be monitored for a time. You have some really naughty influences in your life at the moment, influences that sought you out for the reason of the power you held as a council member. That is ended now," she snaps her fingers and I get the impression that some people met their end with that snap. "Now, you all need to understand, this is my chosen. I will destroy your little council if you make a single move against her. If you make moves to have someone else move against her. There are forces at work that are beyond your comprehension, I will not have centuries of planning thwarted for a boy with no more sense than a teenage mortal."

Scott stands and says, "Who are you that we should do what you say? For all I know you are nothing more than a charlatan, some witch come to sway things for one of her own!"

Lightening flashes in the room and every one of the council members is blown out of their chairs to slam into the wall behind them. As they work to get to their feet she tells them in a voice that fills the room, "I am Hekate! See me and despair! I am the end and the beginning, the Raven of battle, taker of souls and deliverer of fate! This one," she points back at me, "is my chosen. You will let her be or I will end each of you."

Bianca is standing again, she looks to Scott, "You are off the council Scott. Your replacement will be voted in within the next month. Leave now."

The enforcers that visited the house open the door behind the council seating, a door I didn't see until they opened it. Scott looks at them with disdain and turns back to Bianca, "You can't evict me from the counc—" his sentence left unfinished as the enforcers flank him and one claps a hand over his mouth as they pick him up by the arms between them and walk out of the room carrying him. He struggles but to no effect on those guys. We all watch in silence as the door closes behind him.

Hekate turns to me at that point and says, "You are doing so well little one," she steps over and hugs me. I return the hug though I am more than a little shell shocked to be hugged by a goddess. As she releases me she says, "I will be dropping in to see you soon."

With that she just disappears. The council members are seating themselves, with the lady at the end of the right side moving one seat over to take Scott's seat.

Felicity clears her throat and says, "I believe I speak for the council as it stands now, and in the future, when I say that we have decided you will not be a danger to vampire or any other kind. The files will be sealed, with only council members able to look into them and notes will be left for future council regarding the nature of your relationship with the council. You may return to your life and should you find yourself in need of assistance that can be provided by the council, please do not hesitate to contact the council. If that assistance should be needed after we are all gone from the council, instruct them to look in the sealed files room. Here is a direct line with which you may contact us."

She holds out a card and I walk forward to collect it from her. "Thank you, I appreciate your help. Could we add maybe one more note to the file?"

Felicity looks to Bianca, she nods her agreement. "What would you have added to the file?"

"Mikael was my husband from my first life here. He has stalked me for centuries as I reincarnated. Tormenting me with his presence while staying out of reach. When I came back this time, I released the soul tie before I did, because I couldn't stand his games any longer. Since I was turned by him and I realized who he was to me, he has been controlling, tried to murder me because I would not be his, tried just the other day to kidnap me from my home, and I am pretty sure he was behind the explosions that destroyed my home recently. He is obsessed with owning me and will go to any lengths to do so. I have video that one of my roommates took when he attempted to take me. I could share that with you, if that would help. But I need it noted that he will do anything to torment me because he can't own me."

Felicity pulls out her phone, "Send it to me now. We will all watch it and add our thoughts to the note."

I quickly send it to her, she waits till it is fully downloaded and tells me, "Thank you Jasmine. You may go now, the council appreciates your patience. One of the enforcers will be waiting outside the door you entered to escort you home. He will see you all the way to your home as Scott is possibly dumber than he looks."

I bite my cheek to keep from laughing as I nod and turn, walking to the door at the other end of the room. The enforcer that walked me in is waiting outside the room, he holds his arm out to me and I hear the door to the council room close as we walk away.

It is time for my next lesson with Helen, my Lyft driver is driving extra slow. I really wish my new car had survived the bombing of the house. We finally arrive and I tip the driver well, even though I am annoyed at the slow driving. For all I know they are scared of the traffic.

I love walking through the book store, the smells and sounds make my heart happy. I find helen pacing the back room as she waits for me. Her face lights up when she sees me, "Wonderful! Now we can go!"

She grabs some bags from the table and bustles herself out the door and down the hall saying, "Come on slowpoke!"

I catch up to her, "Where are we going?"

I open the door for her as her arms are full of bags and we

walk through the book store in silence as it is pretty packed right now. I open the door to the parking lot and let her go through. She waits till we are halfway across the parking lot to say, "We are going out to a field. You are going to learn calling water. I know you can do some already, but it will be better if you have the practice to do more with it. I feel certain it would have been really helpful to be able to call water into the house and stop the fires raging after the bombs went off."

"Well, yes." She stops at the back of an old Ford Escort with a hatchback and sets the bags down to fish keys out of her purse. Once she unlocks it and has it open I pick up all the bags and stow them gently in the space.

Fifteen minutes later we are on the edge of town, parked in what looks like a driveway to an empty field surrounded by woods. I can smell a creek off in the distance. She opens the hatch and I grab the bags out. She closes the hatch and I follow her out to the middle of the field. Once I set the bags down I see we are in a part of the field that has been used for magic a lot. The plant life has been tamped down from repeated steps and there are rocks set at each of the four direc-tions, along with a larger flat rock in the middle. She sets out all her supplies.

Candles on each of the four directional rocks, a bowl on the center rock. I watch as she walks round the circle, casting her own magical circle as she lights the candles. Once she finishes she turns to me, "Now we can begin. I just needed to make sure that anything excess or unintentional would be dispersed and not cause and damage. Have you called water to you at all?"

"Um, no. Not that I know of. I like to think I would know, but it is possible I missed it."

"You would have noticed. I promise, you would have noticed. Let's sit down. I want you to center yourself. Extend your hands out and cup them, like you would for catching water from a fall. Close your eyes and feel the water. Feel it falling into your hands, cool and clear. Tiny droplets splashing your arms."

Helen goes on, talking in her smoothest voice. She is almost hypnotic and I let myself be carried into the description. I can almost feel like I am in a drenching rain, then Helen gives me a shake. I realize I am in a downpour! She is standing now and dancing in the rain, laughing and giggling. "Look at this! You called in the rain on your first try! This is fantastic!"

I dance with her in the rain for a bit before she tells me, "Now you must disperse it and that may be more difficult. Or maybe you will do it with a wave of your hand." She giggles again.

"Are you going to talk me through it again?"

"Ha! Nope. I want you to do this, I know you can."

I take a deep breath. Ok, I can do this. I am trying to undo it so I guess I need to picture the clouds clearing and the way the earth feels and smells after the rain. What is the word? Petrichor? Yes, that's the word. I sink myself into the feeling of the cooler air after a rain, the smell of a renewed earth, and the misty quality of the moonlight with the water in the air. Opening my eyes I see Helen in front of me, hands together and eyes sparkling, it isn't raining anymore. I am so happy to be finally getting something with some ease.

"Oh Jasmine, you are a natural with water. But now we are going to work to call it from a specific location. In a much smaller amount. Let's sit again. If you place a barrier or air between you and the wet earth you won't have to deal with wet pants all the way home."

"Well that is really fucking handy. How did I never think about this. I bet it would work for keeping fuck boy out of my nose when I have to delete one of them."

"Fuck boy?" Helen pauses, "Honey, are you killing your exes? Not that I blame you but it does become problematic eventually."

"Ha! No. It was other vampires that were trying to kill me or drag me off to see their leader."

"Oh, well, carry on. Speaking of vampires, one of them called me aout you. Said they would cooperate fully if you needed anything and they wanted to make sure I knew as your teacher. What did you get into?"

"Oh, well. Mikael sicced the council on me. Told them about some things I can do that most vampire's can't do." I run a hand across the back of my neck, "Like the magic and that I am immune to the effects of the sun."

I watch as Helen freezes, "Really?"

I nod slowly and watch in amazement as she gets this huge smile on her face. "That is excellent! And handy! There are some places I would like to take you that are quite magical and will aid you in focusing yourself and your magic but I wasn't sure how to get us both there. This makes it so much easier!"

"So you are ok with it? Really?"

"I really am. Now go on, what happened with the council?"

"They called me in and I went through the magic use with them, how you found me in the book store and ended up my teacher. One of them said they knew you and could verify that you had talked about having a new student recently. Then they wanted to question me on the sun thing and Hekate appeared. She told them I belonged to her and fuck off with their bullshit."

"That is a shorter version of what I said but it does convey the idea."

We both jump and look to find Hekate sitting next to us.

Helen claps a hand over her heart saying, "I'm mortal! We die over being frightened like that!"

Looking not at all contrite Hekate apologizes, "I forget that humans are so fragile. I'm sorry, I will try to make a noise next time. The vampire council really got me worked up." She turns to me with a dark smile, "I went to visit Scott. He was not at all happy to see me. But he was smiling when I left."

My eyes widen, I am not sure if she means she put the fear of Her in him, gave him a new smiling hole, or what. I decide to go with the safest answer possible, "I am sure whatever you did was exactly what he deserved."

She laughs and the tension fades, "I think that may have been the most politic answer I have ever gotten from you. I'll allow it this time. I did tell you I would be popping in to see you very soon. You need to know that your earth abilities have not finished coming in. The vines, that was not even entirely you. Part of it was just the earth feeling things stirring and moving in you. Once everything settles in your learning will go so much faster. Back to the earth magic. When that really comes in, you need to be focused on staying calm. Or bad things will happen."

"What do you mean," I ask with some trepidation, "when you say bad things?"

She looks off into the distance for a moment before she answers, "You have all heard the story of Atlantis? Yes?" We both nod, "A chosen one came into their earth element there. While she was being violently attacked. The island was turned into rocks and debris. Very few escaped with their lives. She lived but was devastated that her homeland was gone. It did offer her some cheer to know that her attackers had died in terror."

I swallow though my throat feels dry, "I can understand

how she would feel conflicted. Do I need to be worried that I might sink this place?"

"Probably not. That isn't because you aren't as powerful, it is simply because of the land mass you are on. The one she was on was not made of such stern stuff as this place. But you could definitely level a good country mile or so."

Helen whispers, "Shit."

"Shit is exactly what I was thinking Helen. I- Are you all sure you gave all this to the right person? I feel like this may be a little beyond me."

Hekate laughs, "I am sure. If you were confident in the ability to breeze through everything, then I would be concerned. But you are cautious and don't want to hurt those that you feel don't deserve it. It will be interesting to see if you keep that attitude as you learn more about the world."

Hekate simply disappears after that, leaving us to stare.

Helen says, "You know, I think that is the end of the lesson. Your assignment this week is to practice your meditation and working with water."

* * *

Back home I go sit in the room Eason gave me when we got here. It is a nice room and the view is good. I am feeling unfocused and unprepared. Most of what I have learned to do with my magic is very little.

I am staring out my window when Hekate pops into being before me. It is a surprise but better than her popping up out of sight, "Hello Hekate. What can I do for you? Thank you for appearing in my line of sight, it is appreciated."

"You are welcome little one. I wanted to talk to you without Helen present. She is scared. Very scared. That fear has her dragging her feet about teaching you the things you need to know. I came to teach you a few tricks that may or may not be helpful. I think maybe you have some questions that I can answer about the prophecy and where exactly you fit into everything."

"Really? That would be great. I keep trying to get time to read the prophecy but that hasn't worked out so great and I am pretty sure my copy got turned to ash in the fire."

"I understand." In the blink of an eye the dark and vast power of her is contained and she seems almost motherly. It's a change but I could use some of that, so I am rolling with it as she comes to sit on my bed. "I will leave you with another copy," she waves her hand and one appears on the dresser across the room. "But you will only be allowed to understand certain things at certain times. It is wildly frustrating. However, I can give you sort of an idea."

"Yes please. What the hell am I supposed to be doing here?"

"You darling woman, are going to usher in a new era. Your actions will set off chain reactions that echo around the world. The gist of the prophecy is that you will reject the one that favors the darkness that the world is in currently. He supports the darkness and works to keep it going. As he battles for control of you, a series of events will occur and that will decide how things will fall, so to speak."

"That is less vague. If I had to guess, Mikael is the one I would pick for supports the darkness. I know most people seem to think he is a really great guy but, I think he is probably worse than I want to believe he is. I have to battle him?"

"Yes, but battles aren't always the way they are pictured in the movies humans are so fond of watching. Sometimes the biggest battle is the one you fight within yourself about that person. Nothing in a prophecy should be taken literally. Ever. Even if it says you will eat the eggs of the bird of wisdom, it probably isn't an actual egg and the eating is maybe learning. Maybe. It could be something else too."

"Do I have to choose one person to be with forever after? I don't know if I can."

A light flashes in her eyes, like something just became clear to her and she says, "You don't have to choose just one anymore, do you? The world is moving toward that, it is just a question of whether it swings in the extreme or maintains a balance. You just go where your heart tells you to go. I think it will not let you down."

"That is kind of a relief." I take a deep breath and try to relax a little, "The idea that I had to stick with one person forever to keep the world safe was kind of making me want to run away and hide."

"Well, no need for that. You follow your heart and do what feels right in your soul. That will never steer you wrong."

"Thank you. I feel a little better knowing that. Maybe I can do this. I have a question though, why does so much rest on who I choose to be with?"

"Oh, that is a good one. Creatures of all kinds tend to become more like the company they keep. Or more the image of what that company wants, expects, or demands them to be. In your case, you are kind of a beacon for society. The guiding light of sorts. This doesn't mean you have to be pure and innocent, the world was never meant to be pure and innocent. It mens that your actions are working to right the balance. Things were thrown so far out of balance during the time in which Atlantis fell, some despaired that the balance could be restored. But you, with your attitude and your heart and your courage, you are going to change the whole world for the better just by being you."

"Holy shit. That is the nicest thing anyone has ever said to me."

"I know. And I am so sorry that I couldn't change any of that, I know it was horrendous."

"I—Um. Yeah. But I mean, I got through it. So I can really change things?"

"Yes, you can. Now, want to learn some magic?"

Twenty-One

Jasmine

I slam the book closed and toss it at the end of the bed. Stupid prophecy! No matter how many times I go over any section, even the parts that I think should make sense are not making any damn sense.

I get up and start pacing my room. I'm pretty sure the evil wrapped in light is Mikael. That sounds like him, he always worried about maintaining his image. But the good hiding in the dark, I don't understand. Why does it seem like it is describing more than one person? Helen and Hekate seem pretty convinced it would be the person I ended up with, but I can't have a relationship with more than one person, can I? I mean, is that even a possibility? I know I told Leonidas that I want to hold way off on any sort of commitment, is this why?

Is it even possible?

"Is what possible?" At the sound of a man's voice I jump and spin, my fist shooting out to connect with something before I even see who is behind the voice.

Stepping back and keeping my guard up I realize it is Sebastian! "Oh shit Sebastian, are you ok?" I ask him as I step closer to check the jaw he is rubbing. "You startled me, I reacted before I even thought about who it might be."

He chuckles ruefully, "You know, I have wanted to have your hands on me ever since I first saw you in the hallway at Mikael's, this wasn't exactly how I pictured it."

My hands still on his face, "What? But you turned me down in the kitchen. You never said anything…"

"I haven't really had two minutes to even say hello or get to know you a little better in all this time. One or the other of us has been busy the entire time. I had things with my businesses that needed seeing to and you, well, you had a lot of things to deal with, I figured the last thing you needed was another guy after you."

"Well that depends on how you come after me. I appreciate the thought though. Is your face ok? Sometimes I throw magic in without realizing it."

"My face is fine. But I do have you here alone and your attention on me, maybe we could get to know each other a little better?"

"Before I ask you what exactly you mean by that, I have to tell you I am already in relationships of a sort with Leonidas and Scarlett. Those are not going to stop any time soon, if ever. Knowing that, what do you mean by get to know each other a little better?"

"Well, for right now, I could maybe help you sort out whatever had you talking to yourself? Or take your mind off that completely by having some moderately rough sex."

"Moderately rough? Color me intrigued. Tell me sir, what exactly do you want to do with me?"

He turns and walks to the door, my jaw drops. How could he leave now? Then he shuts the door and comes back. His hands come up to trail his fingers lightly up my arms, when he gets to my upper arms he grabs them and crushes me against his body, tipping his head to one side he whispers into my ear, "That absolutely depends on just what you like. Do you want to be spanked? Like a little choking? Want me to smack that pussy till you cum? Should I tie you up and keep you cumming till you beg me to fuck you?"

My nipples pebble and my panties are soaked from his talk of what he could do, I am so turned on I don't even know what I want to ask for, all of it, some, more. "Unnnh, first, you saying all that in my ear is a huge turn on. Second, I haven't had sex like that. Ever. But I am up for giving just about anything a try."

"Are you now?" He raises an eyebrow and I nod as I bite my lip. I am so turned on right now I can barely contain myself as he says, "Let's start with this. Hands behind your back, hold them there until I say otherwise. And if you want me to stop at any time for any reason, say watermelon."

"Watermelon? Why watermelon?"

"Because it isn't something you would normally say and sometimes during sex no means don't stop. So we need to be really clear when you want me to stop. Ok?"

"I like it. Hands behind my back, delight me good sir."

He chuckles as he drops to his knees. His fingers are nimble as he unfastens my pants and slides them and my panties down my legs. I lift my feet one at a time so he can fully remove them. He plants a single kiss on my mound before he stands and walks over to the bed. He sits and says, "Come, lay across my lap and we will see if you like to be spanked."

My pussy floods at the thought of laying myself over his legs and being spanked by him so I quickly comply, and he tells me to move my arms to the front. I do as I'm told for once and am rewarded with the feeling of his fingertips lightly stroking up the back of my legs. He runs them over my legs, butt, and back till I could scream with frustration. My pussy is dripping and begging to be touched but he is ignoring it.

Just when I think I will scream his fingertips disappear and his hand slaps my ass. I jump and then the warmth spreads and I find I am even wetter. Then another. And another. I am throbbing with need as he rubs my ass gently. His thumb slides over to tease my entrance, I moan as he slides it in. Just a couple light strokes and he spanks me some more. By the time he finishes my thighs are wet.

He slowly slips two fingers into me and I feel my vaginal walls quiver and clench around him. He fucks me slowly with those two fingers as I moan and squirm, "Faster please!"

I hear him chuckle as he continues at the same maddening speed. He puts a hand on my hips to keep me from rocking them and I groan in frustration. Suddenly he withdraws his fingers and lifts me off his lap, holding me in place till my wobbly legs figure out holding me up again. He stands and moves to be behind me. His hands land on my hips and slide up to the bottom edge of my shirt. Grasping it he pulls it up and off of me. I feel his hands at the clasp for my bra, then he is sliding it down my arms to drop to the floor.

He whispers in my ear, "Hands and knees on the bed. Now."

On the bed my back arches of its own accord, thrusting my butt up at him. He takes the invitation, I feel his cock lining up with my entrance. I am so hot with anticipation I think I could combust. That thought scares me back into reality for a moment as I check my magic to reassure myself that nothing is leaking. I tune back into the sensations just in time to feel the glorious stretch as he pushes his way into my hot core. He buries himself in me as his hand trails up my back to grab my hair in his fist. He holds still for just a brief moment before he withdraws almost all the way, only the head is still inside me. My breath catches and he slams back into me as he holds me in place by my hair. He pistons himself in and out of me, the walls of my pussy gripping him tight as he withdraws. His other hand caresses my hip before moving down my belly to rest on my clit. The touch sends electricity through my body.

He never breaks his rhythm as he lifts his hand and brings it back down in a light slap to my clit. I explode into a million stars as he keeps pounding at my pussy. Then he takes two fingers and presses on my clit and the orgasm just keeps going. I think I will die of bliss but he withdraws his hand, pounding his cock into me one more time he holds himself there and as I feel his orgasm happening, it adds another layer of sensation to my still pulsing core.

We both fall forward onto the bed, he slips out of me as he rolls off me and onto the bed beside me. He tells me, "I'll get you cleaned up in just a moment. I didn't expect everything to be so much. I need a minute."

I am not capable of speech yet so I reach over and pat his arm.

A short while later I wake from a light doze to him cleaning his mess and mine from me and I freeze. It is really nice to have someone do that for me. Also a little weird. He finishes up and takes the cloth back to the bathroom where I hear water running as he rinses out the cloth. This is so wild. He comes back over and lays down next to me. I open my eyes to see him looking at mine and I smile.

He says, "I would very much like to do that again sometime if you are amenable. Think you could make some space for me in your harem?"

"Well, you know, I am constantly misbehaving. I obviously need someone to spank me on a regular basis so yeah, I think I can squeeze you in." I laugh, "Get it? Squeeze you in?"

He laughs, "Yes, yes, I get it. Ok, I am going to leave you to your reading now that I have eased your mind and gotten an answer to my question."

"Mind is definitely at ease." I push myself up and roll to a sitting position. "I need to get dressed and do the reading. Ok sir, you take your clothing and be gone with your gorgeous self. I have studying to do."

He chuckles but gathers his clothing and puts it on before he leaves the room with an air kiss blown in my direction. I grab the damned prophecy and crawl under the covers to study it in a much better frame of mind.

* * *

Leonidas

Work is slow tonight. The crew is putting the finishing touches on the house and really they don't need me. They have Daphne laying sod, and she obviously hates it so that has been the most entertaining part of my evening so far. I would rather be spending my time with Jasmine. I know she said she believes me but she hasn't come back by the site since that night.

Maybe she just isn't comfortable coming by knowing that Daphne is working here? Or she is trying to give me space? I should go by there. Wait, what if she is busy? I should call her. Invite her out. Where? Wait!

I think the witch and vampire couple opened a bar recently. I should ask her to go out there with me. We could have drinks, throw darts or axes. Either one sounds fun to me as long as she goes. I could probably be all right with it if she brought Scarlett. If she is going to be with her too I should get used to it. I don't understand how it is that I need her so much I am willing to be one of her partners. I have never been willing to be part of a group before. Maybe it is the immortality? I know we have time, lots of time. It isn't like being mortal, where time is a precious commodity. Picking up my phone I tap the screen a few times and call Jasmine. I just really want to see her.

"Hi Leonidas! How's work going for you tonight?"

"Slow for me, we are just finishing a house tonight. I was thinking about skipping out to play hooky, are you busy?"

"Ooo, what are you thinking about doing?"

"You, if I'm lucky. There is a new bar in town, this witch - vampire couple opened it recently. It's called Just a Little Taste. They serve all kinds of drinks and they have some games. What do you say? Come out with me?"

"I'd love to, that sounds fun. I'll borrow a car for the night. Text me the address?"

"Sure, soon as we end the call. See you in half an hour?"

"Perfect. Bye!"

She ends the call and I head over to talk to Banner. He is my supervisor on this first set of projects and I try to make sure I touch base with him before I do things since he is running it for the most part. "Hey, Banner, I am going to head out for the night. Going to meet up with Jasmine at that new place."

"Just a Little Taste? I heard that place is great. And Jasmine, man, she smells so good I could eat her up."

"I know. I know. She is amazing in so many ways. The way she tastes and smells ends up only being a small part of why I can't stay away from her."

"Well, do right by her. If she shows me the least bit of interest I will forget you are my boss."

"Man, I couldn't even be mad at you. She is awesome. Which is why I am leaving you here to watch the family and I am going to see her. Have a great night, don't call me."

Banner laughs as I head for my truck. I have a duffle bag with extra shirts in the half back seat of my truck and I snatch one out after I get in the truck. Quick shirt change, some cologne and deodorant refresher from the glove compartment and I am set. Firing up the truck and backing out of the drive, I head the truck toward Just a Little Taste.

* * *

Daphne

I stay hunkered down in the shadows as Leonidas drives away. When I can't see his taillights any more I pull out my phone and call Mikael.

"Hello Daphne, what have you got for me?"

"Leonidas is going to meet her right now."

"Oh really? Did he say where they are going?"

"He did, they are meeting up at Just a Little Drink."

"Hmm, perfect. Expect a bonus in your account. Bye Daphne."

* * *

Mikael

Daphne is proving to be much more useful than I imagined it was possible for her to be. I send a text to Vigo, telling him to send her a bonus before I scroll my contacts for another name. Finding it a tap starts a call to him.

"What can I do for you?"

"I have a special assignment. Something that lines up with your skillset."

"Do tell."

"Her name is Jasmine. She is going to Just a Little Taste right now, to meet with Leonidas."

"I know who he is and of the bar. Should be easy to figure out who she is."

"I need her deleted, and him blamed if possible. If not, her deletion will be enough."

"Usual fee plus a rush fee, we don't often do things the night we are hired. It's sloppy."

"Agreed. Payment on receipt of proof as usual."

"Of course."

"Excellent. I look forward to hearing from you and concluding our business."

Twenty-Two

Jasmine

The bar is cute from the outside. I park Quinn's car close to Leonidas' truck and head inside, admiring the neon that spells out the name of the place over and over. Then I realize, it isn't neon at all. That is magic on a loop. How fantastic. I bet these witches could teach me some tricks. The bouncer at the door eyes me and says, "What are you? You smell," he inhales at me, "different."

With a smile I say, "Vampire, but also witch."

He growls, and then sniffs me again, "Go inside before I decide to take a bite of you."

I laugh and lean in to whisper to him, "Better get permission first or I'll take a bite out of you."

Then I walk in the door, leaving him to growl and adjust himself. Just inside I hear some familiar hoots and hollers. Looking around I see some of my old clients from Club Amnesia. One of them asks, "Is the club reopening eventually? I heard the owner doesn't have enough to do it."

"What? What do you mean reopen?"

He says, "Didn't you know?" I shake my head no and he

goes on, "It burnt to the ground last week. During the day while no one was there. Real strange."

"That is strange. Sorry I don't have any information for you. I have to go meet my person, it was great to see you!"

They wave and send me off with good natured shouts. I spot Leonidas across the bar watching me, his eyes hooded and his pose relaxed. I feel really lucky to have these people in my life. Leonidas, gang leader and reason my husband died, setting me free to find this life. I would have none of this if not for him, in a strange way. I wonder if he ever thinks about that? I reach him and he leans forward to wrap me in his arms, it feels like coming home. Releasing me he asks, "Ready for a drink?"

"Yes. Did you know Club Amnesia burnt to the ground?"

"No, what happened? What do you want to drink?"

"Um, they have anything that's got additives? I haven't eaten yet tonight."

"They do. We can ask them to fix you a special. That is where they assess you and create something specifically for you. Since you are hungry, yours would include additives."

"That sounds perfect." Leonidas gets the bartender's attention and she nods at him. He tells me about his drink while we wait. He has some strange combination of whiskey, blood, blood orange, and a dash of grenadine that he is really enjoying. The bartender comes over and I tell her I would like a special please. She nods and I feel a sensation of coolness run through me, it really feels very nice. My eyes drift closed in enjoyment.

When I open them she is staring at me wide-eyed and she whispers, "You are both."

Apprehensive now I ask, "Is that a problem?"

She shakes her head no, "It isn't. Just not usual. The owners would love to meet you. You should come back on a

Monday night. It will be slower in here and they will be here. I know they would love to talk to you."

I tell her I will and she walks off to make my drink. Moments later I am drinking a concoction that tastes like magic and strength and love. I didn't know two of those had flavors but now I know they do and I want this drink every time I drink.

I am telling Leonidas to try my drink when the bar erupts into noise and I feel something stabbing up into my ribs from the left. My drink falls to the floor as I hit the bar. I hear Leonidas roar and I feel the motion of the thing in me stop suddenly. The guys from the club come over and surround me, beating back anyone that makes it around Leonidas. I hear him shout, "Get her out of here! I'll keep you covered!"

One on each side they start walking me to the door. I could move better if I took out the thing, but I'm afraid of letting that much of my blood flow in a public place where just anyone could drink it. Every step to the door is an agony. My lung is on fire, every step stokes the flames. I can hear Leonidas behind me, and I hear the sounds of flesh hitting flesh and other things. The door is so far away. They open the door in front of me and a shot rings out, I feel it tear through my flesh, everything hurts and I can't even tell where it hit me.

The world is roaring around me as the pain sears through my body. They lean me against a wall, I feel them patting my face, "Jasmine! Jasmine! We have to take out the bottle so you can heal, do you understand?"

I struggle to open my eyes, the face in front of me is one of the clients from the club but he looks strange. How does he know I will heal? I nod, everything hurts too much. I feel arms around my shoulders and more around my hips. A hand on my ribs, it hurts so much. Then the thing is pulled out fast, my legs give out and I scream. Something is pressed tight against the spot. The pain is receding. Leonidas is in front of me, "Jasmine, Jasmine baby, we have to pull out the bullet. Just hold on, it will stop hurting in a minute. Jasmine? Open your eyes if you understand."

My eyes don't want to open but I finally lift them, just enough to see Leonidas and a strange group of men around me, but they close again. I can't hold them open.

I hear him say, "Take it out. She knows what we're doing. Get it out of her."

My shoulder burns, it's on fire. I scream and scream, then its gone and the blissful darkness takes me.

I wake to Leonidas dribbling blood into my mouth from a bag. My eyes open now he puts the bag to my lips and I latch on, drinking deeply. I finish two more bags before I feel better. "What happened?"

He shakes his head, "We need to get you out of here. I'll tell you everything you don't know when we get somewhere safe."

I nod, "Let's get out of here. I sure as fuck don't want to hang around tonight."

He helps me stand and I see the guys from the club, they all look a little strange tonight but I'm glad they were here. I know they helped me. "Thank you, all of you. I hope you will forgive me for not sticking around tonight. I don't feel all that great anymore."

One of them steps forward, "No problem. Listen, I know we didn't mention it before, but we know what you are. All of us are shifters. Here is my card," he hands it over to Leonidas, "give that to her when she is better. You call us if you need anything. We are here most nights, so if you need help quick and you are on the move, stop in here. The witches will help you too, they know you were the target tonight."

I nod and Leonidas helps me to his truck. Even after three

bags of blood I still feel a bit wobbly. As he helps me into the truck he tells me, "I'll get Banner to bring the car to the house."

* * *

I am sucking down another bag of blood when Leonidas tells me, "We are being followed."

"Someone is really unhappy about my survival rate so far."

"Seems a fair guess. How are you feeling? I can drive around for a while. But I can't take you home while we have a tail. And we'll need to stop at some point to address this. It looks like only one person on the car, but I can't be sure."

"Um, drive around. I will be fine in a little while, I am nearly healed. There is a lake not far from the house, maybe we could go there."

"And you promise you will run for help if we are outnumbered?"

"No. But I can promise to use my magic to keep anything from touching me."

"I guess that will have to do." He scowls at the rearview, like that will make the other driver go away. I finish the bag I am drinking and grab another out of his cooler. Healing takes a lot. It wouldn't take so much if I was drinking fresh from the source, but bagged is less potent.

We get to the lake just as I am finishing up the last bag. Leonidas drives slowly around it to one of the parking areas. After he parks we get out of my side since it is facing away from the road, watching the headlights of the car while we crouch by the front tire as it drives past us to the next parking area.

By the time the car parks we are in the trees next to the lot it sits in. We can tell there is definitely only on person in the vehicle so we step out of hiding and walk over to the car. As we draw near to the car I realize who it is staring at us from the driver's seat. She gets out of the car and walks to the front of it, stopping to lean against the hood.

Leonidas stalks forward and growls, "Why are you following us?"

Daphne leans in toward him, "I was worried about you! She," Daphne gestures over at me, "has trouble following behind her wherever she goes. You need someone to watch your back and I am always here for you Leonidas, always."

Her voice makes me want to gag, its so sugary sweet. I watch as she tries to hug Leonidas but he is having none of it. He pushes her arms away from him before they ever get anywhere near his neck. But, the main thing I am getting from this interaction is that this is his mess to deal with, it is part of his family business and not any of my business.

"Leonidas, I'm going to go. This doesn't concern me and it looks like she is going to be a whole mess. You come by when you finish cleaning this up, ok?"

He turns to me and takes me into his arms, leaving Daphne huffing. "Are you sure? Are you okay to go that distance alone?"

"I am. And you need to take care of this mess. I'll be fine. Did you get Banner to take that thing by the house for me?"

"I messaged him. He will probably do it later this morning. All right love, you be cautious and let me know you made it home safe. I am going to make sure this is not a problem for us ever again."

I wonder if he is going to end her but I don't really care so I give him a quick kiss and he releases me. I walk off and onto the path that will bring me out near the house.

* * *

Leonidas

I watch as she walks away. I hate this. I can't even take her out for an evening without something fucking it all up. First people trying to kill her and then this bitch. I turn to face Daphne, "What the fuck are you doing here?"

"I told you baby, I just want to keep you safe," she says as she steps toward me and tries to put her hands on me.

I knock her hands away from me, "Don't fucking touch me. You keep your goddamn hands to yourself."

She steps closer, her hands going to my shirt, my pants, they are everywhere. As quick as I smack one away it tries for another piece of my clothing as she whispers, "Don't worry baby, I'll help you forget all about her."

I am horrified and I can't take anymore. "That's it! You are out! I don't know what the fuck your game is but I am done. You are out of the family, don't come back."

She freezes, her head tipped to one side. She smiles and hits me in the gut. I double over, I may not need to breathe but it still hurts to have the air forcibly pushed out like that. I hear her talking to herself, "He'll probably pay me double if I get rid of you completely. The field will be completely open for him." I look up at her just in time to see her foot the instant it connects with my face.

That bitch is shady as fuck but she obviously didn't skip leg day. I drag myself up off the pavement, seeing something moving out of the corner of my eye I duck, feeling the air move over my head as I watch her hit the pavement. "Sucks when you overcommit to a move, eh?"

Daphne comes up from the pavement and charges me as I feel the sun start to rise. I put my hands out to stop her and I open my mouth to tell her to just let it go, but as soon as my hands connect with her shoulders she starts stabbing me with knives she must have had up her sleeves all this time. Before I can push her away she has already stabbed me in a half dozen different places, and I can feel the blood gushing in spots. She shoves away from me and I fall to my knees, trying to press on the heavily bleeding spots long enough for them to seal up. She laughs, "Stupid boy. You lost because you never took the fight seriously. Because I'm just a woman, I can't possibly best a big strong man like you. You all think that and it's your biggest mistake, underestimating me. Now I'm just going to watch you bleed out before I go report your death. It would be nice if you could get on with that."

I chuckle, "Doesn't matter what gender you are, you're still a dumb bitch."

"Oh? Do tell, while you sit there bleeding out because of my knives."

I realize I need some fresh blood to heal this and my only nearby source is about to fry in the sunlight. I launch myself at her, she brings her knives up and gets me in the belly, but I grab her and bite into her shoulder, drawing deeply. I know I have a minute at most before the sun is up and peeking through the trees. Maybe a minute and a half before it immolates her. She twists the knives but my body is stopping the bleeding and she is getting weaker. I feel the sun on my head and I shove her away from me, fire is not how I want to die.

I am still weak from the blood loss, I go down on one knee, bracing my hands on the pavement and breathing heavily. Daphne stands and starts screaming when the first rays of the sun touch her. Her skin starts to shrivel and char, she turns to run at her car as her skin starts to burn. The flames have covered her head when she steps into full sunlight and her body ignites. She makes a couple more steps before her husk falls to the ground, leaving only ashes and fire damage to the front of her car.

That threat eliminated, I am not okay and I need to not be

found like this by passersby. A check of my pockets tells me that I left my damn phone in the truck. It isn't far away but right now it feels like miles. I crawl over to the tree line and pull myself up using a tree. Stumbling from tree to tree I make it to the edge of the other lot. Looking around I don't see anyone in the lot or near it. I try to stumble to the truck but I'm weak and I fall. On all fours I crawl inch by inch to the truck. When my head touches the truck I put a hand up on it and start pushing to get myself up far enough to reach the handle. I know if I pass out now I will be here when the cops show up and they'll take me to a hospital. None of my kind belong in a hospital. I finally reach the handle and I manage to get it open and let myself lean on the truck a minute.

Running my hand across the seat and up to the steering wheel I grab it, this wheel is my lifeline. Working my legs up under me I use the steering wheel to pull myself up just far enough to fall back into the truck. It feels so good to be on something cushioned, even just a little. Can't go to sleep yet! Grabbing the wheel again I pull myself upright before swinging my legs into the truck one at a time. That done I hold onto the wheel with my right arm and reach out with my left to grab the door, resting a moment before I pull it shut as hard as I can. It isn't shut all the way but it will do. I find my phone and pull up Jasmine's number. I put it on speaker and set it on my chest after I hit the call icon.

Twenty-Three

Jasmine

My phone starts to ring and seeing it's Leonidas I answer immediately, "Hey, you on your way?"

"No. I need help."

"What? Where are you?" I ask him as I head for the front door.

"I'm in my truck, it's still parked where we stopped by the lake."

"I'll be right there!" I hit the end button as I run out the front door. I don't even worry about anyone seeing me, I am moving too fast, I would just be a blur for the humans. I am back at his truck in the parking lot by the lake in minutes. Opening the driver's side door I see him laid out across the seat. He is covered in blood.

His eyes flutter open, "Take me home. I have plenty of blood there. That's all I need. Just enough to heal."

I run around to the other side of the truck and open the door, pulling him further over and sitting him up, I strap him in for support. Shutting the door I run back to the driver's side and hop into it. Closing the door I search for the keys, fuck.

They must be in his damn pocket. A quick search and I have his keys pulled out, the truck started and we are on our way.

* * *

We get to his house, I help him in and to the kitchen. Leaving him set on a stool at the island I open the fridge and grab out a bunch of bags. He bites into one and sucks it down. While he drinks I open his shirt, ripping it down the front. I could get all those blood stains out but it just isn't worth it. His wounds are healing but every one of them looks like it was intentionally placed in a spot that a mortal would have bled out from. He finishes his second bag and says, "I told her she was out of the family."

"Is that why she attacked you?"

"I don't think so. At least not entirely. She said something about getting paid double if she got rid of me and left the field open for him."

"Oh fuck, it has to be Mikael. He is the only jackass concerned about getting you out of the playing field, because obviously I am some prize to be won."

He nods as he sucks down his third bag. "I thought as much too. Her attack was a surprise, and the knives even more of a surprise. I was just trying to keep her back and that was my mistake, which she was pretty happy to tell me. If I hadn't gotten the immunity to the sun from you, I would have died anyway. That was what got her, the sun came up and she wasn't prepared."

"Oh fuck, did she burst into flames and all?" I can see his wounds starting to heal and I am relieved.

"It wasn't so much a bursting as a combustion visibly happening. I hate to see anyone go like that but I was not especially sad to see her go as I was bleeding out on the pavement."

"I don't guess you were. You seem to be healing up now, let's get these clothes off you. Before the blood dries and sticks to your skin."

He nods and stands up, his hands start for his pants but I bat them away and unbutton them myself, pulling them gently away from a few wounds. He shrugs out of the remains of his shirt and starts on another bag. He lifts his foot when I tap his leg and I snatch off his boot, sock, and pants on that side before repeating the process on the other side. That done I tell him, "Now go shower. Before I bite you."

He perks up but then shakes his head, "Taking my blood with me," and he grabs a couple more bags as he heads for a shower. I chuckle and pull out my phone to send messages to Chloe and Scarlett. Setting my phone down I clean up, which is really no more than trashing his clothes and the empty bags. I do put the ones he hasn't drank into the fridge, keeping one back for myself because I am still a little off from the attempt on my life earlier.

Sipping on the bag I wander back to my phone, it's odd that neither of them has messaged me back. They are usually still up this time of day. Maybe they went to sleep early. I think I am going to ask Leonidas if I can crash here today. I am just exhausted. I toss the now empty bag into the trash as I walk through the house toward his bathroom.

Twenty-Four

Jasmine

Leonidas is still sleeping deeply when I wake up so I leave him a note telling him I am going home and I jog it. It isn't that far, and being a vampire that is now fully rested and recovered it doesn't affect me to go that distance.

The house is quiet when I arrive, no lights on at all. That's weird but maybe they slept in? Opening the front door I see the house is trashed. Things are broken everywhere. I try to move as slowly as possible as I go through the house, I don't want to miss anyone. These people are my family and if there is one laying here injured I have to help them. My circuit of the house stops when I see the note taped to the fridge. One line that stops my heart.

I have your friends.
   M.

I have to get them back. I don't need to search the rest of the house, I know Mikael is thorough and he has all of them. I pull out my phone as I walk back toward the front door, I need help. Bringing up Helen's phone number I hit the call button. Helen answers, "What's wrong Jasmine?"

"My family. He took my family. I have to get them back. What do I do? I can't let him have them. How do I get them back?" There is a pressure building in me, I don't know what it is but I can't deal with it right now.

I step out the door and see Leonidas pulling up as Helen says, "Come here. He is going to hold them and take good care of them for the moment, it's you he wants. Without them he has no way to force you to his will. Come to the shop. I'll be waiting for you."

"I'll be there in a few."

As I end the call Leonidas says, "I can take you wherever you need to go."

"I need to get to the bookshop now. He took them. He took them all. I have to save them."

He nods and opens his truck door for me.

* * *

At the book store we head directly to the back. Helen is waiting in the practice room, her copy of the prophecy on the table. She looks up as we walk in and says, "I have been studying this. I made it my focus for now. If I am reading it right, this is the first battle. You may want to kill him but he will find a way to slip off and survive. I do see that if you don't get your friends," she sees the look on my face and says, "your family back, everything will go wildly wrong."

The pressure in me is almost unbearable, I push it back down as far as I can. "I know things will go wrong without my family. I need them. I won't be ok without them."

Helen stops her study of the prophecy and says, "I know

dear. You will. You were born for this. You will save them. Just try not to kill him yet."

Leonidas asks, "Is it all right if I kill him?"

"No." Helen shakes her head and goes back to the prophecy, "He has to live this time. He has things to do that will be necessary later."

Leonidas runs a hand through his hair, "Why? What is he doing that no one else can do?"

"It looks like he saves one of you, Jasmine. But it doesn't really say how so it may be something random he does after this fight."

The fuck? This pressure, it feels like I am going to explode but I don't have time for it right now. "Fine. But you said he would find a way to slip off, to avoid dying right? So as long as I don't snatch his head off we should be good, right?"

"Theoretically, yes."

"Is there anything I can do to hide some of what I may do magically?" I ask her as I rub my chest.

"Yes, put a sight/sound shield over everything. Here let me show you how to make one really quick. I can feel you are ready to go. Hekate told me she taught you some 'tricks' and I feel certain that those will be highly useful for you right now. She wouldn't have taught them to you otherwise." Helen goes through putting up this shield, and it is really easy. The practice seems to help with the pressure building, but not nearly enough.

I hug Helen and tell her bye. She tells me, "Be careful. There is nothing in there guaranteeing that you live. You can't keep your friends safe if you die. And don't you think about missing your next lesson!"

I am out the door and moving down the hall before she finishes speaking.

Twenty-Five

ON THE WAY I realize Leonidas has to be prepared for this, he may not realize how far I will go. I look over at him, his face grim as he drives us to Mikael's. "Leonidas?"

"Yes?"

"I need to tell you, this is going to be a shit show. If he wants me, then at the very least I am going to have to seem like I am going with him."

"I don't like that plan. Do we have anything else?"

"No. No we don't. He wants me and I am probably going to need to go with him. I need you to not stand in the way. I am begging you to trust me, to have faith in me. I will do everything I can to make sure I come out of this safe, but I need you to make sure they get away safe. I will take care of the rest. Can you do that for me?"

He growls, "I can try. But I won't be fucking happy about it and I sure as shit cannot pretend it."

"I wouldn't ask that." I rub my chest as the pressure within builds, I feel almost like it is choking me. "Just get everyone out when the time comes."

He nods as we stop in front of Mikael's. There is a large

group of people out front, armed to the teeth. "Shit. Get out on this side. Hold on to me and whatever happens, don't let go," I tell Leonidas as I step out of the truck.

He slides over and lands behind me, "Why do I need to hold on?"

The wind is picking up as I unleash a little of my magic, "Because I can't do little or complicated magics yet, whatever I do ends up big. I don't want us to get separated."

"Ah fuck!" He says as he grabs me round the waist and plants his feet. With him attached I raise my arms and let the magic flow even as I hear the guns fire. A massive wind comes from behind me, knocking us both to the ground. The people in front of Mikael's house are thrown everywhere. I close my eyes as I struggle to stop the flow of magic. It is boiling up out of me and stopping it is a lot harder than it should be. It still feels like there is so much pressure inside me. I just have to get this fixed, then I can figure that out.

I manage to stop the flow, the wind dies down. Leonidas and I get to our feet, and we both see the few people behind Mikael's fence struggling to their feet. Leonidas says, "Mind if I take care of them?"

"Please do." I watch as he leaps over the fence from standing in front of it and decimates the people on the other side. I follow more slowly, my body feeling impossibly stretched by the power straining to get out.

I get through the get by simply pushing it open, I don't have the strength to hold the tide of power back and jump over fences. Leonidas joins me, "Are you ok?"

"Yes and no. My magic is doing something strange. It's like there is too much of it. It's fine. Just make sure you get everyone out safe. Ok?"

He presses his lips together but nods.

Twenty-Six

Jasmine

We walk into Mikael's house, he is there waiting. A huge curtain has been hung across part of the entry, I am afraid of who or what may be hidden behind the curtain. Mikael is waiting, he has a chair in front of the staircase. He stands as we enter, "Jasmine! Welcome! I began to wonder if you would even show, I thought perhaps I had collected the wrong people. But here you are." He hold up a remote control and pushes a button. The curtain drops, revealing my family all held in a giant cage. "All I have to do is press this button and they go free. Or I press this button and they fry. You get to choose, all I want is you. You come to me, be with me as was meant to be all this time and they go free."

I look at my friends in the cage, they are telling me don't do it. My heart breaks with love for them. They know he would kill them and still they want me to go free. Deep breath, "Mikael, you were kind in the past. Will you allow me to say good bye to Leonidas?"

"Of course my love, I can be merciful. Say your goodbyes, he won't be allowed to see you again."

Leonidas is stricken, "Don't do this. Please, there has to be another way."

I whisper to him, "I told you it might be like this. You promised."

He grabs me and kisses me hard, I kiss him back with everything in me as hot tears escape my eyes. He pulls back and whispers, "You better come back to us."

He releases me and walks to the cage as I turn and walk to Mikael. The pressure within me is painful. Every breath hurts. My steps are measured but I make it to Mikael, he grabs me and crushes me to him. I cry out, the pain is beyond what I can bear. Mikael silences me by pressing a punishing kiss to my lips, bending my body back as he presses forward. I hear the door to the cage clang open and then Mikael stops punishing me with his lips as he drags me to his office. I don't resist, I can't resist. Everything hurts, my power is clawing its way free of the cage that is my body. I feel him kick the door closed as he tosses me down. The lock engaging is so loud in my ears, and then the dam breaks.

* * *

Leonidas

I am helping them get out of the cage when I hear it. The ground is rumbling. Oh shit, "Guys, we have to get out of here now. You've got to run, she is going to bring the whole place down!" The rumbles grow louder even as I shout at them to run.

Chloe yells as we make it out the front door, "How far should we go?"

"I don't know! At least off Mikael's property! Till we don't feel the ground shaking!"

* * *

Mikael

Jasmine doesn't struggle at all as I take her to my office. Once in there I kick the door shut and let her fall while I lock it. Picking up my sweet Jasmine, I turn her in my arms to face me, I can resist her charms no longer. I kiss her hard, so she knows I am still unhappy with having had to go this far before she came to her senses. My hands roam her body, I let the control for the cage fall to the floor. Her body is just as luscious as I remember.

I should have gone this route to begin with, she's so much more pliable. "Jasmine, I've missed you so much! I love you, and I will never let you go again." Grabbing her ass I press her hard against my body, "Jasmine, how could you not miss what we had together?"

I feel a rumble as I kiss my way from her neck down to her cleavage. I shift my hands so I can push her shirt to one side and the entire house shakes. Freezing in place I wait to see if there is another. The next rumble makes some of the bricks from the fireplace fall out and shatter.

I look at Jasmine in my arms and she is nearly glowing with magic. I realize the rumbles must be coming from her, "Jasmine, you stop that this minute!" Slapping her hard I yell, "I will have your friends brought right back here and I will spend my days torturing them while you watch! Now you stop this right now!" I give her another slap but it has no effect. Her eyes roll back in her skull and her arms float out away from her body as her face turns up to the ceiling. I release her and she floats, never even looking around. The house is shaking even harder now, I have to get out of here before it comes down around my ears.

I back up to the door, unlocking it and opening it slowly. As soon as it is fully opened I bolt for the back of the house. The kitchen is a shambles as I sprint through it, the door has come open as the frame is warping with the twisting of the house. I dive through it as it starts to collapse in on itself and hit the ground, tucking and rolling. I roll onto my feet and start running. I don't stop running until I reach the edge of the yard.

Turning back I watch as the house shakes and rumbles, twisting in ways I didn't know a house could twist. It falls in on itself. I don't see Jasmine floating out. I guess her magic didn't protect her from the consequences of her actions. That really is a shame. I adored the body she was in this time. Well, perhaps she will be gifted with an even better body next time? One can only hope. Still, such a shame she had to go like that.

I turn away from the rubble that was my home for so long and start walking. Pulling out my phone I call Vigo and tell him where to meet me.

Twenty-Seven

Leonidas

We are a block away from the house before we realize the ground isn't shaking here. Stopping we start walking slowly back. We come to the edge of the property in time to see the house shake its last before the whole thing just collapses in on itself.

Come on Jasmine, I watch for movement anywhere in the rubble. I start praying to all the Goddesses that she is still alive in there. Not seeing any movement, I can't take it anymore. I run over and try to find the area he dragged her off to before we high-tailed it out of there. Careful, but as quick as I can I start pulling debris away and chucking it. Just let me find her, oh please let me find her safe is my prayer as I dig. Scarlet and Sebastian have joined me in this area while Chloe, Eason, Asher, and Quinn are a little farther out.

Scarlett shouts, "Hand! I found her hand! Oh, thank fuck its attached! Help me dig her out!"

Sebastian and I work together to pull the debris over

Jasmine away as Scarlett holds onto the Jasmine's hand, repeating over and over, "We've got you, we're getting you out of here. Just hang on, shit, Jasmine, wake up please. Talk to us, let us know you are ok."

Finally she is completely uncovered and Scarlett is hugging her to her body, crying and begging her to wake up. I hear sirens in the distance. "Fuck, we need to get out of here before the cops arrive." I turn back to Jasmine to pick her up but Sebastian has her cradled in his arms and is picking his way out of the pile of rubble. I don't like that he has her, but it works. "Come on, my truck is over here. I'll take us all home. My house has space and it isn't trashed."

Sebastian looks over at me, "It's only the downstairs that is trashed. None of the fighting happened upstairs."

"No one showed up at my house to kidnap anyone or kill her. I think it is the safest, because if Mikael knew where it was he could have had the note delivered there."

Scarlett cuts in, "Shut up both of you. Sebastian, get in the fucking truck. Leonidas, you too. Don't make me tell either of you twice. The rest of you, get in the back. I am riding in the middle of these idiots for Jasmine's sake."

Well, I am an idiot. I do as the lady says and get in the drivers seat. She slides across the seat from the passenger side and helps Sebastian settle Jasmine as he climbs in. The truck bounces lightly as the rest hop into the back and lay down. I start to feel the coming of sunrise, I have to get them home now, not everyone here is immune to the effects of the sun.

* * *

Jasmine - three days later

. . .

The darkness is sending me back. It was warm here, comforting. I didn't have to worry that I would be stuck with Mikael forever to protect my family. It won't hold me any longer though. The nudges to the surface are getting harder. I tell the darkness, "I just want to stay with you, to sleep in peace with you."

I feel something like arms come round me, holding me. Rocking me. Comforting me like a mother would her child. The darkness releases me, ghostly hands on my shoulders, one moves to cup the side of my face briefly. Then I am nudged to toward the surface once again. Resigned to my fate I allow myself to float to the surface.

Opening eyes that feel dry and sensitive, I blink them slowly to get things going again. I hear voices whisper around me, it sounds like my family but it can't be. Mikael has me, they won't be allowed near me.

My eyes begin to focus and my hearing is clearer. I swear I just heard Leonidas say, "She's waking up!"

My eyes gravitate toward the voice and I gasp, it looks like Leonidas standing next to me. I let my eyes move around the room, hoping this isn't some cruel trick being played by Mikael. Scarlett stands next to him, her face radiant with joy as she smiles at me. Chloe is next to her, hugging Eason for all he's worth. Quinn and Asher are standing there, arms crossed and grins on their faces. Sebastian stands past them, next to me. I can't believe they are all here. What are they doing here?

I work my jaw a bit and ask, "What's going on?" Because something big must have happened, there is no way Mikael would let me have them near. "Am I dead?"

They all laugh and Scarlett says with a grin, "No honey, you aren't dead. You scared the hell out of us, but you are still here. If you decide you don't want to be here, maybe just let us know. You don't have to bring the whole house down to escape."

"What? Why would I do that?"

Leonidas gets to eye level with me, why am I in a bed? He says, "You brought Mikael's house down on top of the two of you after you sacrificed yourself so your family would be safe."

Well, I'm awake now. "I'm sorry. I think my hearing isn't quite right just yet. It sounded like you said I brought Mikael's house down. That can't be right."

Sebastian leans a bit to be in my line of sight, "You did. The entire house is a pile of sticks now."

"Holy shit." I sit myself up and scoot back against the pillows that Leonidas and Sebastian piled behind me, "The last thing I remember is sending you to get everyone else out of Mikael's house and a lot of pressure in me. What happened after that?"

Chloe says, "Mikael grabbed you as soon as you got near him. He hit the button to release us and dragged you away to his office. You looked really weird, floppy. You weren't struggling or anything. Then the house started to rumble and shake. We got out like you wanted, but came back when we realized that this was only happening to the house. Nothing else was having an earthquake. As soon as everything settled we started searching for you. You were unconscious when we found you but we brought you home and poured blood down your throat, since choking wasn't really a concern. We have been doing that for the past three days."

"I was out for three days? Fuuuck. What about Mikael? Did you find his body? Or did he escape?"

"Honestly," Sebastian says, "we quit looking after we found you. But, the news didn't say anything about finding a body so either he turned to dust or he escaped. Dust looked more likely."

Leonidas scowls at him, "I told you, he isn't dead. Helen said he would find a way to slip off."

Sebastian scowls right back, "Do you believe that or are you just saying that to disagree with me?"

"Both!"

Shaking my head I hold my hands up palms out toward each side of the bed, "Guys, not now. We can measure your dicks some other time. For now, I just need a shower." I look around, "Where am I?"

Leonidas grins, "My house. I put you in another room to keep the peace, but you can come to my room for a shower, it has the best bathroom."

Sebastian lift a brow at him but lets it pass. Scarlett rolls her eyes, "They have been like this since we pulled you from the rubble. It's been a trial. I am so glad you are awake. It was a major discussion every time you were due to be fed. Now that you are fully awake, I am going to bed for a few days. You are welcome to join me there any time you wish. Leave these two idiots to their own devices for a while."

I thank Scarlett and make her come over for a hug before she leaves the room. Everyone else insists on getting their own hug and by the time they all leave the room I am in tears from all the love. As I move to stand I realize I am naked. I look at the two of them, "Nobody thought to mention that I was sitting here with my tits out this whole damn time?"

They both smirk and Sebastian says, "Why would we deprive ourselves like that?"

"Ugh. Men." I stand and snatch the blanket from the bed and wrap it round myself. I take a step and nearly fall but the guys each grab an arm to keep me from toppling. "So I used magic to bring the house down with an earthquake? Guess that is why I am still off balance. Ok, let me try this again but slower and more deliberate. Let go guys, but catch me if I fall."

They don't look happy though they release me. I take a careful step and make it. Followed by another and another, all the way to Leonidas' room where I stop at the door to tell them, "I need to shower alone guys. I appreciate the concern so much more than you know, but I need to do this alone. You are welcome to listen for a fall," their faces perk up, "from out here." I step back into the room and close the door.

* * *

In the time since I woke up from my dream in the darkness my magic has grown while I am training hard. The earth magic that exploded from me the night I destroyed Mikael's house is leveling out and most days I don't make the house rumble. Our house is being rebuilt by Leonidas and his crew, they decided it would be much bigger than what we had bought originally. Karen down the street hates it but she hasn't been able to stop a single permit from going through.

Everyone insists that Mikael must have died that night, but I can still feel him out there. I know he is alive and when he comes for me, I'll be ready.

* * *

Author's Note

I hope you are enjoying Jasmine's story as much as I am enjoying the writing of it. The next book in this series will be out in December 2021. I know two months is a really long time, but it's as fat as I can get it out of my brain. While you wait, have you read my Fate's Chronicles series? The first book, A Vampire's Fate, is free on all retailers. I also wrote a novella about Fate's origin story called Fated for Halloween.

You can get the novella free for signing up to my monthly

newsletter. The link for that is at the end of the preview Fated for Halloween.

The Fate's Chronicles series is completed now, the final book released on July 27, 2021. I hope you have enjoyed this book and that you will enjoy the rest of the series as well.

Thank you for reading what the voices in my head told me!

Rhiannon

P.S.

Reviews really help other people decide whether or not to read a book. If you feel a way about this book, I would sincerely appreciate a review.

About the Author

Rhiannon writes steamy paranormal romance. She is an avid reader of many authors in a variety of genre though she tends more toward paranormal.

She has three former pound puppies that she dotes on and three daughters that she adores.

Rhiannon has lived in multiple states though she is currently residing in North Carolina. Wandering, witching, and reading with her puppies and husband are what she does when she isn't writing.

To learn about what is happening in Rhiannon's world and get loads of pupper cuteness, sign up for the by using the QR code below to visit my website.

Also by Rhiannon Futch

The Daughter of the Moon series-
Selena Rose, Daughter of the Moon Book 1
Thorns of the Rose, Daughter of the Moon Book 2
Heart of the Rose, Daughter of the Moon Book 3
The Fate's Chronicles series
A Vampire's Fate
A Vampire's Treasure
A Vampire's Dream
A Vampire's Chase
A Vampire's Fight
Fated for Halloween - only available via email signup
The Belancore Witches of North Carolina series
Witchy Ever After
A Witchy New Year
My Witchy Valentine
Sin series
Sin on a Dark Knight
Sin on a Broken Heart
Sin on a Burning Heart
Sin on a Vengeful Heart
The Vampire Kings Series
Mercy of the Vampire King
Shame of the Vampire King

Pursuit of the Vampire King

Prey of the Vampire King

Reign of the Vampire King

Coming Soon

Love and Vampires Series

Olivia's Fall

Olivia's Prison

Olivia's Flight

Olivia's Family

Warriors of the Old Gods

A Dream of Blood

A Dream of Wolves

A Dream of Stone

A Dream of Ravens

A Dream of Bones